Guardian's Mission

An Anna Gabriel Novel : Book 5

Georgia Wagner

Text Copyright © 2025 Georgia Wagner

Publisher: Greenfield Press Ltd

The right of Georgia Wagner to be identified as author of the Work has been asserted in accordance with the Copyright, Designs and Patents Act 1988

All rights reserved.

The book is copyright material and must not be copied, reproduced, transferred, distributed, leased, licensed or publicly performed or used in any way except as specifically permitted in writing by the publishers, as allowed under the terms and conditions under which it was purchased or as strictly permitted by applicable copyright law. Any unauthorised distribution or use of this text may be a direct infringement of the author's and publisher's rights and those responsible may be liable in law accordingly.

'Guardian's Mission' is a work of fiction. Names, characters, businesses, organisations, places, events, and incidents either are the product of the author's imagination or are used fictitiously. Any resemblance to actual persons, living or dead, and events or locations is entirely coincidental.

Contents

1. Chapter 1 — 1
2. Chapter 2 — 15
3. Chapter 3 — 25
4. Chapter 4 — 34
5. Chapter 5 — 48
6. Chapter 6 — 67
7. Chapter 7 — 91
8. Chapter 8 — 98
9. Chapter 9 — 115
10. Chapter 10 — 133
11. Chapter 11 — 141
12. Chapter 12 — 159
13. Chapter 13 — 174

14.	Chapter 14	195
15.	Chapter 15	208
16.	Chapter 16	224
17.	Chapter 17	234
18.	Chapter 18	244
19.	Epilogue:	258
20.	What's Next for Anna?	264
21.	Also by Georgia Wagner	266
22.	Also by Georgia Wagner	268
23.	Also by Georgia Wagner	270
24.	Want to know more?	272
25.	About the Author	274

Chapter 1

Investigator Petrov's boots splashed through puddles on the dock. The rain hammered against his coat. Water dripped from his nose and chin. The air smelled of salt, brine, and diesel fuel. And in the distance, cranes loomed like fishing giants dropping their lines against the black sky, their lights casting long shadows across the concrete.

Petrov pulled his collar higher, a useless gesture. The rain found its way in. His socks were wet. His feet were cold. He could see the shipping container at the end of the dock, blue paint peeling from rusty metal. Police lights flashed against its sides, alternating red and blue. Red. Blue. Red. Blue. Each beat like a stop-motion frame capturing the drama unfolding in their glow. Officers stood around it, their faces ghostly in the harsh lights.

Sergeant Kuznetsov spotted him and nodded, saying nothing. This was unusual for Kuznetsov. The man talked too much—always. But not tonight.

Officer Kozlov bent over behind the container. Retching sounds pierced the rain as Petrov approached, and as he angled his approach, he saw the young officer's dinner splattered on the wet concrete, already being washed away by the rain. Nobody moved to help him.

"The body. It's in there?" Petrov asked.

Kuznetsov nodded. His eyes were red. His hands shook as he cupped his mouth and lit a cigarette.

"How bad?"

"Bad." Kuznetsov's voice cracked. "Very bad."

Petrov took a deep breath and exhaled slowly. He'd seen it all in twenty years: stabbings, shootings, strangulations, dismemberments. Nothing surprised him anymore—or so he thought. Since his wife's illness, he'd spent all his grief and horror at home. There was simply no more left for the terrors that came with his occupation.

He approached the container. Its door hung open. A thin beam of light cut through the darkness inside, but the smell hit him first: blood and decay. Something wrong had happened here.

GUARDIAN'S MISSION

Petrov reached for his flashlight. He clicked it on and stepped forward, then stopped almost immediately. His shoes stuck to the floor, a tacky peeling sound reverberating inside the shipping container: blood, thick and congealing... and far too much of it.

A crime scene technician stood inside, camera in hand. His face was green as he nodded at Petrov, but he quickly stepped aside.

Petrov's flashlight beam swept across the container floor. When it stopped, it illuminated what remained of a human being.

"Shit," the investigator whispered as he rubbed at the stubble on his chin.

The victim's arms and legs were spread in a giant X, but the shadows were all wrong. They were too separated, light slicing between the extended limbs and the shadows they cast on the floor beneath them—as if he were hovering off the ground.

Petrov blinked, doing a double take, flickering his flashlight back and forth as he tried to make sense of what his eyes told him.

The victim hung suspended in the center of the container. Four steel cables stretched from each limb to the container walls. They were taut, thick industrial strength lines—the kind used on construction sites. The body didn't touch the floor, didn't touch *anything*. It just hung there in empty space, nearly three feet off the ground.

Petrov stepped closer. His flashlight beam caught the victim's face: white hair, not gray, not blond. It was pure white...like snow. Cropped short against the skull, the line dividing scalp from skin nearly invisible. That was when the investigator noticed the victim's skin was pale—too pale. It had been drained of blood, drained of life.

The eyes stared at the ceiling. They were pink eyes—an albino then. Those eyes remained open, unfocused and sightless, like a ghost's eyes. They reflected the flashlight beam in that unnerving way a corpse always does, with no dilation or flinching, almost as if he was looking at a painting instead of a person. And those two small points of light held the dull gleam of his torch, as unfeeling as glass marbles in the darkness of the container.

Crouching, Petrov tilted his head to look at the floor beneath the suspended victim. Blood had pooled beneath the body in a perfect circle. Almost black against the metal floor, it had dripped from multiple wounds. He could see precise cuts now, dozens of them, each one shallow. None looked fatal on its own, but together... Together, they had drained the life from the victim, drop by drop.

The victim's clothes hung in tatters, shredded by whatever blade had slit open his flesh: a sharp one by the look of things. But the victim's chest was bare—exposed.

"Do we have an ID?" Petrov asked at last, standing once more. His voice echoed in the metal box sounding too loud to even his own ears.

"Nothing." Kuznetsov stood in the doorway. He wouldn't come inside. "No wallet. No phone. No identification of any kind."

Petrov circled the body. The cables didn't sag, there was no sign they were giving at all. Someone had used a winch to pull them this tight—to suspend the victim so perfectly—and Petrov grimaced as he wondered whether the autopsy would show the limbs coming out of their joints from the tension. He hoped whoever had done this at least had the decency to kill the man before stretching him like some medieval torturer... but he doubted it. The work was precise, the position calculated. The victim faced the door, ready to be found... a macabre gift of sorts.

"Time of death?" Petrov asked.

"Medical examiner says between thirty-six and forty-eight hours ago." Kuznetsov 's voice was flat. Monotone. "Temperature in the container makes it hard to be precise."

The victim's hands were bound with a thin, sharp wire. It had cut into the flesh and blood had dried around the bindings—the feet too. Same wire. Same technique.

Petrov leaned closer, this time bending over the body to examine the victim's neck. A thin line circled it, not deep enough to kill, just enough to hurt, to control. As he looked closely, his flashlight caught something on the victim's forehead: letters. They were carved into the skin and fresh. The blood still looked wet.

"The container?" Petrov asked, staring at the letters in close scrutiny.

"It arrived yesterday morning on the Estonian freight ship *Kursk*," Kuznetsov called out. "Nobody checked it until tonight. Dock worker heard something. Thought maybe rats. Found this instead."

"Get me more light," Petrov ordered.

A technician brought over a portable flood lamp and switched it on. Harsh white light filled the container and the victim's pink eyes seemed to glow in the brightness, unflinching, burning with the light as if looking into the face of God.

"Who does something like this," Kuznetsov muttered, staring at the corpse as he also took note of the letters engraved on the victim's skin.

Petrov didn't reply. Whoever had done this knew how to use a knife. That was all there was to say, and saying it aloud felt foolish. He grimaced, speculating on what drives a man to do a thing like this.

"Someone wanted to extract information…" he speculated.

"They tortured him," Kuznetsov whispered, nodding as if this summation was not only a description but an explanation.

"Obviously," Petrov growled. "And he…" Petrov gestured to the dead man, "was strong-willed. Very strong. Or very scared of revealing the information."

"Terrible…"

Petrov turned to scowl at Kuznetsov . "Whoever did this to him was stronger still."

Just then, a commotion erupted outside the container. Voices shouted. Warnings were muffled by the container walls, causing Petrov and Kuznetsov to both look out in sudden alarm.

"Get down!" someone screamed. "On the ground, now!"

Petrov rushed to the container entrance, rain lashed against his face. The dock lights created a wall of brightness beyond the container's shadow. He squinted, blinking away water.

Officers formed a half-circle, weapons drawn. Their shouts overlapped, urgent and tense. Fingers hovered near triggers. Their attention was fixed on a figure emerging from between two stacks of containers.

A woman. She walked toward them with a steady pace, unhurried. Her arms extended outward from her body. Her palms were open—empty. And the rain plastered her clothes to her frame, water streaming down her face.

"Stop right there!" Kuznetsov bellowed, his service weapon aimed at her chest. "On the ground! Now!"

She didn't stop. Didn't run. Didn't show fear. Her footsteps echoed on the wet concrete. *Tap. Tap. Tap.* Measured. Deliberate. She moved with a strange grace, like a predator. Her eyes scanned the officers and assessed them. It was a look Petrov knew well and respected for what it implied about her. She was calculating: distances, angles, threats. She was formulating a plan to escape if this did not go her way... and deciding how many of them she'd have to hurt to do it.

"I said on the ground!" Kuznetsov's voice cracked. His hands trembled on his weapon.

Petrov stepped forward to support his partner, and the rain lashed over him as he left the shelter of the container's walls. "Last warning!"

The woman's gaze locked onto him. Her eyes were a sharp and keen green, penetrating like a predator's eyes—like a tiger sizing up if he was a threat or just meat. Her face was all angles: high cheekbones and a strong jaw, but it was broken up by a celestial nose that might have been at home on a model instead of this steel blade of a woman. Water dripped from a streak of pure white hair among black strands. The rest of her hair was black as the stormy sky above the port.

"I'm unarmed," she said. Her voice carried across the distance, but he still quirked an ear to see if he had understood her. Was that an American accent? It was confident whatever it was, clear in tone if nothing else despite the pounding rain.

Petrov noticed her stance: military. The way she held herself, the way she assessed her surroundings, even the scarring of old wounds visible on her neck and disappearing beneath her collar screamed out that she was a professional—maybe even spec ops.

"On your knees! Hands behind your head!" Kozlov had recovered from his sickness, but his weapon shook in his hands.

The woman stopped ten meters from the nearest officer. She looked at the shipping container, at the body inside. Her expression revealed nothing: no shock, no disgust, no surprise.

"I'm going to lower myself to the ground now," she announced. No fear in her voice. Just calm certainty. "I killed that man."

She spoke calmly, matter-of-factly.

The officers tensed. Petrov just stared, uncertain if he'd heard correctly. Fingers tightened on triggers. Petrov held up his hand, signaling them to wait.

The woman knelt on the wet concrete, rainwater soaking up through her pants more than it already had. She placed her hands behind her head. Interlocked her fingers. It was textbook compliance—perfect form. She knew the procedure.

"Face down," Petrov ordered.

She complied and lowered herself to the ground: cheek against the concrete, arms extended to her sides, palms up, and ankles crossed. Again... textbook. She was making herself as non-threatening as possible.

Kozlov moved forward, handcuffs ready. His steps were hesitant, but Petrov nodded. Two more officers flanked Kozlov, weapons trained on the woman.

"Careful," Petrov said.

Kozlov approached next, knelt beside her, grabbed her right wrist and pulled it behind her back. He snapped the cuff in place, then just as quickly moved to her left wrist. The metal clicked. The woman didn't resist, didn't speak, didn't move.

Kozlov patted her down. No weapons. No ID. Just wet clothes and a body that felt like coiled steel beneath his touch.

"Clear," he announced, his voice steadier now.

"Get her up," Petrov ordered.

Kozlov and another officer pulled the woman to her feet. Water ran down her face. Her expression remained blank, empty. Her eyes found Petrov's and held them. There was no fear there, no remorse... nothing.

"Name?" Petrov asked.

"Anna Gabriel."

American. Definitely American.

"Why did you kill him?" Petrov gestured toward the container.

"He had information." Her voice was flat. Emotionless. "I needed it."

"And did you get it?"

"Yes."

Petrov studied her face. The steadiness of her gaze, the controlled breathing, the military posture even in handcuffs. He didn't know what was going on here, but he believed her, and the acknowledgement of that belief sent a shiver up his rigid spine.

"Take her to the station," he told Kozlov. "Interrogation room one. I want two officers with her at all times. No one speaks to her until I get there."

Kozlov nodded. He and the other officer led Anna Gabriel away. Her steps remained measured, unhurried, as if she were leading them rather than being led.

Petrov watched her go. Something wasn't right. Confessions didn't happen like this. Killers didn't surrender themselves at crime scenes—not killers capable of what had been done inside that container. And yet... from the look in her eyes, the way she carried herself... there was a part of him that had no doubt she *could* have been the killer.

"She's lying," Kuznetsov said beside him. "Has to be."

"Maybe." Petrov wiped rain from his face. "Maybe not."

He turned back to the container and the suspended body. He muttered under his breath, shaking his head.

Petrov's phone vibrated in his pocket. He pulled it out and checked the screen. It was a message from his wife, a short phrase. *Coming home soon?* He didn't reply. For a moment, his mind left the madness around him, turning to his own personal hell. She was making solyanka; she had the strength for that at least. But the day was coming when she wouldn't... and a day beyond that when there would be no more texts... no more lights on when he returned home. Only the cold and the quiet. The sickening fear in the thought removed him from the icy horror of what transpired under this evil rain, if only for a moment.

He reached into his coat and found his cigarettes. Pulling one out, he straightened it between his fingers. It was damp, but not so far gone it wouldn't catch. Lighting up despite the rain, he inhaled deeply, enjoying the burn as it cleared his head and returned him to the present.

Why would she confess? Why would she walk up to a dozen armed officers? Why surrender when she could have disappeared?

The albino in the container had been tortured by an expert: someone who knew how to inflict maximum pain, someone who understood human endurance, someone trained. Military. Special operations, maybe. The woman, Anna Gabriel, moved like a soldier. She held herself like one. American special forces? CIA? Something else?

Petrov took another drag. The cigarette hissed as raindrops struck the burning tip. He glanced at the shipping container again, at the body suspended inside it and the pool of blood beneath it.

Flicking the cigarette into a puddle, he stomped on it as he moved towards the waiting vehicle.

The strange woman was watching him through the window—those same predator eyes following him the whole way—and he felt his skin crawl.

Something evil had come to his city. And Anna Gabriel was at the heart of it.

Chapter 2

Anna strode slowly through the Russian precinct. Her wet boots squeaked against the linoleum floor, and water dripped from her clothes, forming small puddles with each step. The cheap flooring glistened with the fallen moisture and reflected back the fluorescent lights buzzing overhead—harsh and unforgiving. From above and below, they cast the group's faces in a sickly yellow glow.

The station smelled of cigarettes, wet wool, and cheap coffee: old coffee, burnt coffee—the kind that had been sitting on a hot plate for hours. Officers moved around her, and their voices echoed off concrete walls. The building was Soviet-era construction, functional and utilitarian, with no wasted space but also no aesthetic consideration.

Astrakhan Port Authority Police Station. Southern Russia. Caspian Sea region. Anna had memorized the location during mission prep. It was a strategic position—a major shipping hub and a gateway between Europe and Asia. It handled a high volume of cargo with low security standards, making it perfect for moving things that shouldn't be moved.

Anna cataloged her surroundings: two exits visible from her position; the main entrance behind her; an emergency exit to her right; Seven personnel in the main room—three uniformed officers, two in plain clothes; two administrative staff. And most were armed with standard-issue Makarov pistols. There were also three security cameras—one in each corner of the ceiling. One was planted above the booking desk. They were all older models—analog, not digital.

And then, of course, there were the handcuffs pressing into her wrists—not too tight. Officer Kozlov knew his job: restraint without unnecessary pain, a professional. She could work with a professional.

Her gaze drifted to a wall map of the Caspian coast. Ports were marked in red, shipping lanes in blue. The Volga Delta spread like veins across the northern coastline.

"Move," Kozlov said in Russian. His hand pressed against her upper back, but the pressure was not forceful, just a guiding touch.

Anna complied. Her mind ran threat assessments, escape routes, and the force required. Casualties were likely if she tried to press an escape at this point, and she dismissed the thoughts. It wasn't the plan—not yet anyway. She'd surrendered on the dock for a reason.

As she glanced down at her hands and more specifically, the blood under her fingernails. It had dried by now, despite the damp, forming dark crescents against her skin. It was the albino's blood. And that was fitting. What *he'd* said had led to this encounter.

"This way," Kozlov directed her down a narrow hallway of gray walls—scuffed from years of shoulders brushing against them. Anna took in the doors on either side as she passed: interrogation rooms, storage, evidence lockup.

This was all normal so far, but as they went deeper into the building, Anna's mind continued to turn. There was a non-zero chance she was being led to one of the darker, all-concrete rooms in the basement or furthest hall—the sort with a metal drain in the floor for easy cleanup inevitably kept in Soviet-era facilities for discreet 'state business'. If that was the case, she'd have to make a choice—likely one that meant being a lot less cooperative than she'd been.

Two officers accompanied her now, one in front, one behind. This was still standard procedure for high-risk detainees, and Anna idly recognized that they must consider her high-risk. Good assessment.

Anna kept her face blank, revealing nothing. The mission parameters remained clear in her mind: obtain the information, verify its authenticity, ensure containment. Phase one had been completed in that shipping container. Phase two was in progress. The rest would follow.

The officers led Anna to 'interrogation room one,' a small, windowless box with concrete walls painted institutional green decades ago. The paint had faded to the color of old moss. A metal table bolted to the floor dominated the center of the room, and two metal chairs faced each other across its scarred surface. A single light fixture hung from the ceiling, protected by a wire cage. The bulb inside cast harsh white light that left no shadows to hide in.

A camera peered down from the upper corner. Its red recording light blinked steadily—watching. A large mirror covered most of one wall, a standard observation setup with two-way glass. Someone would be behind it soon, if they weren't already.

Kozlov guided Anna to the chair facing the mirror. She sat down without resistance, her movements fluid despite the handcuffs. The metal seat was cold through her wet clothes, and water continued to drip from her hair, forming a small puddle beneath her chair and pinging off the metal in fingertip taps. Her boots had lost much of their grime on the walk here, but muddy prints still showed themselves on the concrete floor—port grime, oil and salt.

"Wait here," Kozlov said, an unnecessary instruction. Where would she go?

The door closed behind the officers with a heavy metallic *clank*. The lock engaged with a solid sound, reassuring to them perhaps, meaningless to her. Anna knew fourteen ways to exit a standard Russian interrogation room. Not that any of them mattered now.

She settled into the chair, her posture perfect—back straight, shoulders relaxed, feet flat on the floor. She controlled her breathing with slow and measured inhalations. In through the nose. Out through the mouth. Her heart rate remained steady, sixty-two beats per minute: normal for her.

Twenty-seven minutes passed.

She counted every second. There was no use second-guessing her plan now. This was expected, too. They were making her wait, a standard tactic to build anticipation, raise anxiety, and make a suspect more pliable to interrogation. It wouldn't work on her.

At last, the door opened, and the man she recognized as investigator Petrov entered. He had changed his clothes and dried off. Now in a dark gray suit with a professional white shirt—no tie, though—his coat was draped over his arm.

The door closed behind Petrov with a *click* that echoed in the small room. He hung his coat on a hook by the door, movements deliberate, unhurried. His eyes never left Anna, and in a way, they mirrored her own: assessing, calculating, professional eyes—eyes that had seen the worst humanity could offer and somehow kept looking anyway.

He circled the table once before sitting. His shoes made soft sounds against the concrete floor. Not quite a prowl but something close to it: a predator sizing up potential prey—or perhaps weighing another predator who had strayed into his territory.

"You're American," he said, settling into the chair opposite her. It was not a question, merely a statement.

Anna didn't respond. Her eyes met his without blinking. The green of her irises seemed unnaturally bright under the harsh interrogation room lights.

"Your Russian is decent. Military trained, I'd guess." Petrov placed a manila folder on the table between them. It remained closed. "But you're not here officially. No diplomatic calls. No lawyers demanding your release."

The clock on the wall ticked. Seconds stretched between them.

"You confessed to murder," Petrov continued. "Walked right up to armed officers at an active crime scene. That's not normal behavior, even for Americans."

A small pool of water had formed beneath Anna's chair. The dripping from her clothes had slowed to an occasional drop. The sound punctuated the silence between Petrov's words.

"The man in the container," Petrov leaned forward, "was tortured. Systematically. Professionally. Hours of pain before death. That requires training. Experience." His eyes narrowed. "It requires a certain kind of person."

Anna remained still. Her breathing hadn't changed—sixty-two beats per minute, steady.

"Why confess?" Petrov asked. "Why not just disappear?"

Anna's voice, when it finally came, was calm and measured. "I need to make a phone call."

Petrov's laugh was sharp and humorless. "A phone call? This isn't American television, Ms. Gabriel. You've confessed to torture and murder on Russian soil. You're not entitled to anything."

"One phone call," Anna repeated. "Then I'll tell you everything about the man in the container."

"You'll tell me everything now." Petrov's voice hardened. "Starting with who he was."

"I will tell you *one* thing now. And then you're going to give me that phone call," Anna replied, her voice no less firm, but infinitely calmer than Petrov's. And before he could reply, she went on.

"His name was Viktor Orlov. Former FSB. Specialized in chemical weapons development before going private sector eight years ago." Anna recited the facts like reading from an internal dossier. "He sold secrets to the highest bidder. Recently, he worked as a body double for a former employer of his—a man known as the Albino."

Petrov's expression didn't change, but something flickered in his eyes: recognition.

"The phone call," Anna said again. "One number. You can monitor it. Record it. Whatever security protocols you need."

Petrov studied her for a long moment. The clock continued to tick, punctuating the length of his consideration. "And if I refuse?" he replied slowly.

"Then I say nothing further."

"We have ways of making people talk too," he said, though by the tone it was clear he expected she knew this already.

Anna didn't blink. "It won't work."

"You think so?"

She always hated this part: when men thought she was bluffing. She wasn't—she simply wanted to save the time of the attempt. Anna let out a disappointed sigh, as if Petrov were a student giving an incorrect answer when he ought to know better.

"I know so." Anna's eyes remained locked on his, unwavering. "You can try. But you'll waste time you don't have."

Petrov leaned back, studying her face. She could see the way his eyes went to the scarring visible at her collar, to the white streak in her hair. He was seeing it now, the complete absence of fear in her posture.

"The body in the container," he said slowly. "There was a message carved into his forehead. Do you know what it said?"

"'Pretender,'" Anna replied without hesitation. "Carved with a ceramic blade. Non-metallic. Doesn't set off detectors."

Petrov's eyes narrowed slightly. He hadn't mentioned that detail to anyone outside the crime scene. She was telling the truth about the killing, at least.

"This phone call," he said. "Who would you be contacting?"

"Someone who can make an offer."

"An offer? What type of offer."

She shrugged. "Turn off that camera, and I'll tell you."

A longer pause. "What *sort* of offer?"

She looked him dead in the eyes. "An offer for *you*."

He blinked.

"I've done my homework, Petrov. I know about your wife's medical bills." She spoke quietly, staring at him as if peering into his soul. Petrov gaped at her like a wounded fish.

Anna leaned in now, her voice hard. "Time is of the essence. Give me my call, and I'll change your life."

Chapter 3

Petrov felt the blood drain from his face. For a moment, the interrogation room seemed to tilt. The air became too thin.

"Don't look so surprised, Investigator." Anna's voice remained flat, emotionless. "Information is currency in my line of work. Your wife's condition. The treatments in Germany that Russian insurance won't cover. The second mortgage on your apartment. The loans from colleagues."

Petrov's hand curled into a fist beneath the table. His knuckles whitened.

"Turn off the camera," Anna said again. "Give me the phone call. What happens next benefits us both."

His jaw tightened. Twenty years on the force—twenty years playing by the rules. Mostly. Petrov had made small compromises here and there, nothing that kept him awake at night—until Natasha's diagnosis, until the doctors said the only treatment was experimental...expensive...foreign.

This woman murdered someone, he reminded himself. *Tortured him first. For hours.*

The question remained, resounding in his mind. *Why?*

But Natasha's face swam before his eyes, the pain etching deeper lines around her eyes each day. The medication barely touched it anymore.

Petrov stood abruptly. His chair scraped against concrete. Without a word, he walked to the corner of the room, reached up, and disconnected the camera's power cable. The red recording light blinked out.

"Five minutes," he said, returning to the table. "That's how long before someone notices and comes to check."

Anna nodded once. "Your cell phone."

Petrov hesitated, then pulled his phone from his pocket. He placed it on the table between them. Anna glanced down at her cuffed hands, and Petrov produced a key, unlocking the restraints.

They fell to the table with a metallic clatter as Anna rubbed her wrists briefly, then picked up the phone. Her fingers moved across the screen with practiced efficiency, dialing the number from memory. Eleven digits, an international number. She activated the speaker function and placed the phone on the table.

Three rings. A *click*.

"Yes?" It was a man's voice with an American accent, clipped and professional.

"Verification code seven-three-nine-alpha-echo-tango," Anna said.

A pause. "Verified. Status?"

"Phase one complete. Phase two in progress. I have Investigator Petrov with me, Port Authority Police."

"Understood." The voice shifted slightly, addressing Petrov now. "Investigator, I represent an organization with mutual interests regarding Viktor Orlov and his associates."

Petrov's eyes narrowed. "What organization?"

"One that prefers discretion." The voice remained calm, measured. "We're aware of your financial situation. We can offer immediate assistance. Five hundred thousand euros transferred to your account in Zürich. Another five hundred upon successful completion of our arrangement."

Petrov's breath caught. A million euros? It was enough for Natasha's treatment—recovery and rehabilitation too. It was still a gamble, but now it would be one he would have the buy-in to make. It could be enough to save her, enough to stop waking up each night in cold sweats, terrified she wouldn't be there in the morning.

"What arrangement?" His voice sounded distant to his own ears, as if someone else were speaking.

"Simple cooperation," the voice replied. The connection crackled with static as rain drummed against the station roof above them, a steady percussion that seemed to match Petrov's accelerating heartbeat. And as the line cleared again, the mysterious voice continued. "We need Ms. Gabriel processed through your system in a very specific manner."

Petrov's eyes flicked to Anna. Her face remained impassive, unreadable.

"Explain." Petrov's mouth had gone dry.

The voice continued, smooth as glass. "You will process Anna Gabriel as a male suspect. Complete documentation change. Gender, physical description, everything. You will ensure she is remanded to the men's detention facility at Astrakhan Central Prison."

A beat of silence filled the room. Petrov blinked, certain he had misheard.

"That's... impossible," he finally managed. "There are protocols. Medical examinations. Other officers. Cameras."

"All manageable obstacles with your cooperation," the voice replied. "Ms. Gabriel will assist with the physical transformation. Your job is to ensure the paperwork reflects our needs and that she reaches the correct facility."

Anna leaned forward slightly. The fluorescent light cast harsh shadows across her angular face, emphasizing the sharp cheekbones. "We've paid the right doctor. It's all arranged. We have someone who'll alter digital records from the outside. We just need your cooperation."

"You want me to falsify police records," Petrov said flatly. "Commit fraud. Risk my career."

"We want you to save your wife," the voice corrected. "The first transfer of funds will occur within one hour of your agreement. The funds will arrive before Ms. Gabriel reaches the prison transport. Consider your position carefully, Investigator."

Petrov's gaze drifted to the two-way mirror. Who might be watching? Listening? The camera was off, but that didn't mean they were truly alone.

"The processing area security footage will experience technical difficulties," Anna said quietly, reading his thoughts. "The night shift is understaffed. Three officers total, including yourself. Two can be managed."

"Managed how?" Petrov's voice hardened.

"Both are your subordinates. They won't question you."

He stared. She was right. How did they know so much about his precinct?

He shifted uncomfortably, glancing once more at the camera. He shivered and then turned, opening the door. He stepped into the hall, glancing left and right. No one was watching.

Petrov closed the door behind him, leaning against it for a moment. His heart hammered in his chest. A million euros. For Natasha. For a chance. He wiped sweat from his brow with a trembling hand.

The hallway stretched empty before him. They were still on the night shift, a skeleton crew. It... could be manageable. His shoes squeaked against the linoleum as he walked to the observation room next door. He needed to know who was watching. Who had heard.

He opened the door to find Officer Kozlov slouched in a chair, headphones on, scrolling through his phone. The young officer jumped to attention when he saw Petrov.

"Sir! I was just—"

"The audio," Petrov interrupted. "Is it working?"

Kozlov's face flushed. "No, sir. Technical issue. I reported it to maintenance, but..." He gestured helplessly at his phone. "Night shift."

Petrov nodded slowly. No coincidence. They had arranged this too. How far ahead had they planned? How deep did their resources go?

"And the camera?" he asked.

"Just went out, sir. I was about to check—"

"I disconnected it," Petrov said. "Testing a theory with the suspect. Stay here. Monitor visually. I'll handle the interrogation personally."

Kozlov nodded, relief evident on his face. He didn't want to be near the woman who had done what they'd found in that container, and Petrov couldn't blame him.

Back in the hallway, he thought of Natasha's face when the doctors had delivered the diagnosis, the way the light had seemed to leave her eyes... the way she tried to smile for his benefit, even through the pain.

He thought of the man in the container, suspended and tortured. Who was he really? Viktor Orlov? Or was that another convenient lie to further Ms. Gabriel's plans? Regardless of who he had been, what information could possibly justify such brutality?

Petrov returned to the interrogation room. Anna sat exactly as he'd left her. Perfectly still. Perfectly composed. His phone lay on the table between them.

"Your wife can begin treatment next week," Anna said without preamble. "The clinic in Munich has already been contacted. They're expecting her."

Petrov's mouth went dry. "How—"

"We're thorough." She gestured to the phone. "Check your email."

He picked up the phone. An email notification showed on the screen from an address he didn't recognize. He opened it with a shaking finger.

Confirmation of a patient slot at the Hoffmann Clinic. Natasha's name. Diagnosis. Treatment plan. Everything arranged. Paid in full.

"This is real?" He could barely form the words.

"As real as the body in the container," Anna replied. Her green eyes fixed on his. "The first transfer has been made. Five hundred thousand euros to your account in Zürich… minus the expenses of the initial treatment."

He bit his lip, heart pounding. A decision. He had to make a decision.

He stared at the email—the confirmation of the money—swallowing nervously. They'd thought of everything. And if he said no… If he backed out now after everything he'd seen… Did he really want to end up in a container himself?

Petrov released a slow breath, and nodded.

"Wait here a moment… Mr. Gabriel."

Chapter 4

Anna sat stoically in the chair as the buzzer shaved her head. She stared at the blank, gray wall.

"We have to be quick," Petrov was muttering. "Don't flinch."

Anna didn't flinch. She remained perfectly still as her black hair fell in clumps around her feet, covering the concrete floor of the small processing room. The white streak—her most identifying feature—disappeared among the rest. The electric buzzer hummed aggressively against her scalp, its vibration traveling through her skull and down her spine.

Petrov worked methodically, his movements precise despite the tremor in his hands. The door was locked, the security camera disabled. "Technical malfunction," he'd told the night technician. Just one of many that would plague the station's systems tonight.

"Almost done," he murmured, more to himself than to her.

Anna's mind was elsewhere—calculating time frames, contingencies, extraction points. The Albino's double had talked before he died. He had screamed what she needed to know between pleas for mercy that never came... a location within Astrakhan Central Prison.

The Albino thought he could hide in a Russian prison. He was running his operation from behind the walls of a supermax.

No way for her to get to him.

That's what he'd thought.

The buzzer fell silent. Petrov stepped back, examining his work. Anna's head was now completely bald, the shape of her skull revealed—elegant and dangerous, like the rest of her. Without hair to soften her features, her face looked even more angular, almost alien in its sharpness.

"The binding," Anna said. Her voice remained flat, emotionless.

Petrov hesitated, then reached into a duffel bag on the floor. He removed a roll of medical compression bandage. "This will hurt."

Anna stood and began unbuttoning her shirt. Petrov turned away, uncomfortable with her clinical efficiency. She stripped to the waist, revealing a torso mapped with scars—bullet wounds, knife slashes, burn marks, a battlefield recorded on skin.

"Turn around," she instructed.

Petrov complied reluctantly. Anna had already begun wrapping the bandage tightly around her chest, compressing her breasts against her ribcage. Her breathing became more shallow as she pulled the material taut.

"Tighter," she said, holding the end of the bandage out to him.

"You won't be able to breathe properly."

"Tighter," she repeated.

Petrov took the bandage and pulled it firmly, wrapping it around her torso several more times before securing it with hard-plastic clips. Anna's silhouette had changed, becoming more masculine, more linear.

"The clothes," she said, nodding toward the duffel.

Petrov produced a plain white undershirt, too large for her frame. Anna pulled it on, then a standard-issue blue prison uniform shirt that hung loosely on her shoulders. Next came baggy prison pants, the waistband rolled several times to keep them from slipping off her narrow hips.

It wasn't perfect. But it didn't have to be.

They'd greased the right palms. And once inside the prison, it wouldn't matter what the other prisoners thought. Not after she made an example of a couple of them.

She would handle it like she always did: clinical, direct. She already knew the mission. Now it was the matter of following through on it.

"Complete the processing," Anna said quietly, giving the uniform a final tug to ensure it was secure. "We need to move. The doctor at the facility who does the exams is only on shift until midnight."

Petrov nodded. The man looked equal parts relieved and terrified. She didn't blame him. When he woke tomorrow, this would all feel like a dream—until he saw the confirmation email once more, the string of zeros in his Zurich account's new balance.

The investigator led Anna through the station's back corridors, away from the main processing area. Her movements had changed—shoulders squared, stride lengthened, center of gravity shifted. If this was going to work, the next several hours had to leave a lasting impression. She couldn't overlook anything that might give her away.

The prison transport vehicle waited in the loading bay, engine idling. A single guard stood beside it, smoking a cigarette that glowed orange in the darkness. Rain continued to fall, creating a curtain of water between the station door and the vehicle.

"Papers," the guard said, flicking his cigarette into a puddle as they approached.

Petrov handed over the falsified documents. "Prisoner transfer to Astrakhan Central. Special processing."

The guard scanned the paperwork, eyes flicking briefly to Anna. The harsh security lights cast deep shadows across her shaved head and angular face. In the baggy prison uniform, with her bound chest and altered posture, she passed a cursory inspection.

"Dangerous?" the guard asked, nodding toward Anna.

"Very," Petrov replied. "Isolation cell recommended."

The guard grunted, signing the transfer form. "What'd he do?"

"Killed a man. Tortured him first."

"Sick bastard," the guard muttered, handing back the paperwork. He opened the transport vehicle's rear door. "In you go."

Anna climbed inside without hesitation. The interior was divided by a metal grate—prisoners on one side, guards on the other. The bench was cold metal, bolted to the floor. No windows. No comfort. Just bare functionality and the lingering smell of disinfectant covering something worse.

"Hands," the guard instructed.

Anna extended her wrists. The guard secured them with heavy steel cuffs connected to a chain that ran to shackles around her ankles: standard prisoner transport protocol. She had expected it, planned for it.

The door slammed shut with a metallic finality. Through the small, reinforced window, Anna saw Petrov standing in the rain, water streaming down his face. Their eyes met briefly before the vehicle lurched forward, pulling away from the station.

Anna settled against the hard metal bench. The driver and another guard sat on the other side of the grate, neither paying her any attention. Their radio crackled with routine communications: weather reports, road conditions... nothing that concerned her.

The vehicle's suspension groaned as it navigated the potholed streets of Astrakha, rain hammering against the roof like distant gunfire. Anna closed her eyes, visualizing the route to the prison. Seven kilometers. Approximately fifteen minutes in current weather conditions.

She regulated her breathing despite the painful restriction of the binding around her chest. Measured inhalations. Controlled exhalations. The pain was information, nothing more. It couldn't touch the core of her.

The mission parameters scrolled through her mind. Infiltrate Astrakhan Central Prison, locate the target and extract information—eliminate if necessary. The Albino had hidden himself where he thought he couldn't be reached, a place too well guarded, too dangerous.

He was running his arms trade through couriers from behind those prison walls and had managed to get himself placed in solitary, protected by the armed guards.

She was going in unarmed, a woman in a man's world.

The transport van jostled over a pothole, slamming Anna against the metal wall. She absorbed the impact without changing her expression. Her mind reviewed distances, mapped corridors she had only seen in blueprints. Astrakhan Central Prison had been built in the Soviet era—a maze of concrete and steel designed to break men's spirits.

But she knew the Albino was there—not as a prisoner under his real name, but hidden within the system under a false identity, protected by corrupt officials, untouchable to most.

But not to her.

The van slowed, turning onto a gravel road that crunched beneath its tires. The sound of rain diminished as they passed under something—a covered entry point. The vehicle stopped. Engines died. Doors opened at the front.

"End of the line," one guard announced, pulling open the rear door. Rain-soaked air rushed in, carrying the smell of wet concrete and rusted metal.

Anna squinted against the harsh floodlights that illuminated the prison's receiving area. Gray concrete walls topped with razor wire rose on all sides. Watchtowers loomed at each corner, searchlights sweeping across the compound in regular patterns.

Two prison guards approached, their faces impassive beneath the brims of their caps. Water dripped from the edges as they evaluated their new charge.

"Special processing," the transport guard explained, handing over Petrov's paperwork. "Direct to medical, then isolation."

One of the prison guards—older, with a face like weathered leather—reviewed the documents. His eyes narrowed slightly as he glanced at Anna, then back to the papers.

"Murder case?" he asked.

"Torture and murder," the transport guard confirmed. "Port Authority jurisdiction."

The older guard nodded. "We'll take him from here."

The chains rattled as Anna was pulled from the van. The rain was stopping, but water still dripped from the edges of the processing area's metal roof. Each drop echoed against the poured stone floor with musical precision.

"Move," the younger guard ordered, prodding her forward with a baton.

Anna walked toward the main building, her shackles forcing a shuffling gait. Steel doors hissed open automatically as they approached to the sound of mechanical locks disengaging. Security systems activated with electronic whines as cameras tracked their movement.

Even at the door, the prison smelled of industrial disinfectant, sweat, and desperation. Fluorescent lights buzzed overhead, casting everything in a sickly green-white glow. Their footsteps echoed down the long corridor—two steady rhythms from the guards, one shuffling cadence from Anna's shackled feet.

They passed through three security checkpoints, each requiring identification verification from the guards. No one looked too closely at Anna. She was just another prisoner—another number. Her face remained passive, revealing nothing of what was happening behind her eyes.

At the medical processing center, a tired-looking doctor glanced up from his desk. His white coat was stained with coffee at the collar, and deep circles shadowed his eyes. The small room smelled of antiseptic and cigarettes. Medical equipment—much of it outdated—lined the walls on metal shelves.

"Another one?" the doctor asked, not bothering to hide his annoyance. "It's nearly midnight."

"Special processing," the older guard replied, handing over the paperwork. "Direct order from Port Authority."

The doctor scanned the documents, his eyebrows rising slightly. He glanced at Anna, studying her shaved head and angular features. Something flickered in his eyes—suspicion, perhaps—but was quickly replaced by resignation.

"Fine." He sighed, standing up. "Remove the restraints for the examination."

The younger guard hesitated. "Sir, this prisoner is classified as highly dangerous."

"And I'm classified as highly irritable after a fourteen-hour shift," the doctor snapped. "I can't examine him properly in chains. That's protocol."

The guards exchanged glances before the older one nodded. He produced a key and unlocked Anna's restraints. The metal cuffs fell away, leaving red marks around her wrists.

"Wait outside," the doctor instructed the guards. "Standard privacy protocols."

The older guard frowned. "We should remain—"

"Outside," the doctor repeated firmly. "Unless you want to explain to the warden why medical protocols were violated on your watch."

The guards withdrew reluctantly, closing the door behind them. The moment they were gone, the doctor's demeanor changed. He moved to a cabinet, unlocked it with a key from his pocket, and retrieved a small envelope.

"You must be the package," he said quietly, his back to Anna. "They said you'd arrive tonight."

Anna remained silent, assessing. The doctor turned, envelope in hand.

"Five thousand euros," he continued, tapping the envelope against his palm. "That's what they paid me to look the other way during your processing. No cavity search. No questions about your physical anomalies." He smiled thinly. "Must be important, whatever you're here for."

Anna stepped closer, her movements fluid and controlled despite hours in restraints. "Just do your job, doctor."

He shrugged, tucking the envelope into his coat pocket. "Already done. As far as my records will show, I've completed a standard intake examination on prisoner number 6173, male, age thirty-two, no significant medical issues." He gestured to a form on his desk, already filled out and signed. "Simple."

Anna nodded once. The doctor walked to the door, then paused.

"Whatever you're doing in here," he said without turning around, "I don't want to know. But Astrakhan Central isn't kind to newcomers—especially the isolation wing." He glanced back at her. "That's where you're headed, yes?"

The doctor's words hung in the air between them. Anna kept her face impassive, but her mind cataloged his warning alongside everything else she knew about Astrakhan Central Prison.

"The isolation wing was built differently than the rest," the doctor continued, voice dropping lower. "Stalin-era construction. Cells carved into bedrock beneath the main facility. No windows. No natural light. The walls weep moisture when the temperature drops." His fingers drummed nervously against the doorframe. "Men go mad down there. Not just from isolation. Something about the place... it gets inside you."

The doctor shook his head, eyes distant. "Last month, a prisoner in isolation chewed through his own wrist. Arterial spray painted patterns across his cell wall before the guards found him. Another one gouged his eyes out with his thumbnail." He turned back to Anna. "The guards say it's just what happens when you lock men away from light and human contact. I think it's something in the walls themselves, something that whispers."

He straightened his stained coat. "Your medical check is complete. The guards will return you to isolation processing." With that, he opened the door and summoned the waiting guards.

The older guard eyed Anna suspiciously as he reattached the restraints. The metal clicked cold against her skin.

"Medical processing complete," the doctor announced, handing over the signed forms. "Prisoner is cleared for facility placement."

Chapter 5

The guards led Anna deeper into the prison complex. Each step took her further from the outside world, through layers of security designed to keep society safe from those within these walls.

They descended, one level below ground then another. The air grew colder, damper. The lighting changed from harsh fluorescent to bare bulbs in wire cages spaced at irregular intervals. The corridor narrowed. Concrete gave way to older construction—stone blocks fitted together, their surfaces slick with condensation.

The isolation wing entrance loomed before them—a massive steel door set into the stone wall. A guard station stood beside it, manned by two officers who acted more like carved statues than men, their faces blank from years of service in this underground realm.

"New arrival," the older guard announced, presenting the paperwork. "Direct to isolation by order of Port Authority."

One of the station guards scanned the documents, then shook his head. "Not possible. Two of the units are still closed. No room."

Anna tensed. If she ended up in gen pop this was going to get complicated *fast*.

The guard escorting her frowned. He waved the form and said something too quickly in Russian for her to catch. But the guards outside the isolation wing were all shaking their heads adamantly.

Anna kept her eyes down, trying not to look up. It wouldn't take too much scrutiny for someone to start asking questions about her appearance, and if she wasn't placed in isolation, then she would be mixed with the prison's general population. Then it wouldn't be a matter of *if* she was caught. It would be a matter of *when*.

Shit.

She had no negotiating leverage here. In chains, she had no options.

Double shit.

She kept her face downturned, rapidly considering her dwindling options.

As she stood there, listening to the guards mutter at each other in Russian, trying to pawn her off as someone else's problem, she found her mind flitting back.

It had taken her hours to get the albino's body double to talk. He'd been scared of the Albino. Very scared.

But when he'd revealed where the Albino was hiding, Anna had believed him. Casper and Waldo were with Beth, hiding out in a safehouse on the shores of the Caspian sea.

The guards continued their heated debate. Anna caught snippets—something about overcrowding, bureaucratic mixups, and a flooded section of the isolation wing. The older guard who had escorted her kept jabbing his finger at the paperwork, his face reddening with each passing minute.

Finally, the isolation wing guard slammed his palm on the metal desk. "*Nyet!* Two cells flooded yesterday. Electrical issue. Won't be fixed until next week. Take him to max security gen pop. Cell block D has space."

The older guard's face twisted with frustration. "This prisoner is classified as—"

GUARDIAN'S MISSION

"Not my problem," the isolation guard cut him off. "Orders from the warden. No exceptions until repairs are complete."

Anna's mind raced through contingency plans. General population complicated things: more variables, more witnesses, and more potential threats.

The guards turned her around roughly, marching her back up the damp stone corridor. The shackles chafed against her ankles as she shuffled alongside them. They ascended one level, then moved horizontally through a maze of corridors. The prison was a labyrinth of concrete and steel, designed to confuse and disorient. Anna memorized each turn, each doorway, building a mental map of her surroundings.

Cell Block D loomed ahead—a massive open space with cells stacked three levels high along the perimeter walls. A central guard station panopticon provided a 360-degree view of the entire block. Metal walkways with railings connected the upper-level cells. The space echoed with the sound of distant voices, coughing, the occasional shout or laugh quickly silenced.

Night lockdown was in effect. Most prisoners were in their cells, though a few trustees moved about, cleaning or delivering items under guard supervision. The overhead lights had been dimmed to their nighttime setting, muddling the long shadows cast across the concrete floor.

The processing guard at Cell Block D—a heavyset man with a bushy mustache—looked up from his newspaper as they approached. "What's this?"

"New prisoner," the escorting guard explained, handing over the paperwork. "Isolation's full. He's yours now."

The block guard scanned the documents, his eyebrows rising. "Torture and murder? And you're bringing him to gen pop?"

The escorting guard shrugged. "Warden's orders. No room in isolation."

"Fine," the block guard sighed, stamping the transfer form. "Cell 217. Upper level, north side. Two occupants already."

Anna's restraints were removed for the final time. The metal cuffs had left angry red marks around her wrists and ankles. She rubbed them absently, eyes scanning the cell block. Approximately sixty cells were visible. She could see their occupants shuffling back and forth, but in her minds eye she was already filtering them into a more useful category.

Threats. All of the cells were full of threats.

She let out a slow, quiet exhalation. She'd dealt with dangerous people before, but never when she was trapped in such close quarters. At any moment, she might find herself hopelessly outnumbered, outmuscled, and all the training in the world wouldn't let her brute-force her way out.

The block guard led Anna up a metal staircase to the second level. Their footsteps rang out against the steel, echoing through the cavernous space. Most cells were dark, their occupants sleeping or pretending to. Occasionally, eyes gleamed in the darkness, watching the new arrival with predatory interest.

"Home sweet home," the guard muttered, stopping before cell 217.

He rapped his baton against the bars once, a perfunctory warning to those inside, then pressed his thumb against a biometric scanner. The lock disengaged with a heavy mechanical clunk. The cell door slid open just enough for a person to squeeze through.

"In," the guard ordered, gesturing with his baton.

Anna stepped inside. What other option was there? The cell was approximately three meters by two meters. Concrete walls on three sides, bars on the fourth. A metal toilet and sink unit occupied one corner, offering no privacy. Three bunks were bolted to the walls—two on one side, stacked, and a single on the opposite wall. The air smelled of sweat, mildew, and cheap soap.

The door slid shut behind her with a sound of finality. The lock re-engaged automatically. The guard didn't look back as he returned to his station, keys jangling at his belt.

Anna stood motionless in the center of the cell, eyes adjusting to the dimness. The only light came from the corridor outside—a faint glow that cast more shadows than illumination. Enough to see that two of the bunks were occupied.

On the bottom bunk to her right lay a massive figure. He slept on his back, one arm flung across his chest, the other hanging off the edge of the narrow bed. His breathing was deep and regular, punctuated by the occasional soft snore. Even in sleep, his face maintained a perpetual scowl, eyebrows drawn together over a broken nose that had been reset poorly.

His exposed arms and neck were a canvas of prison tattoos—not the random scrawls of amateurs, but the deliberate, meaningful marks of the *vor v zakone*, the Russian thieves-in-law. Stars on his shoulders marked him as authority. Orthodox church domes on his chest signified time served. A skull on his right forearm suggested he'd killed for the brotherhood.

He was dangerous. But predictable. The thieves-in-law followed a code. They could be reasoned with, if you understood their rules and showed proper respect.

The upper bunk was empty—hers, presumably.

On the single bunk across from them lay her second cellmate. Unlike the giant on the bottom bunk, this one slept like a soldier in a war zone—on his side, facing the door, one leg drawn up slightly, ready to move at a moment's notice. His breathing was so shallow it was almost imperceptible.

He was lean, wiry rather than muscular, with a shaved head that gleamed faintly in the dim light.

Where the first man's body told a story of brute force, this one spoke of speed and precision. He had fewer tattoos, but their placement was significant—a spider's web on his neck, visible just above his collar, marking him as an assassin. A single teardrop beneath his right eye. The placement and design suggested former military or intelligence work gone wrong. This one was unpredictable. Insidious. The more dangerous of the two.

Neither had woken when she entered—or they were pretending to sleep, evaluating the newcomer before revealing themselves. She decided this was the more likely option given the guard's baton rap before opening the door.

Anna moved silently across the cell, placing one foot on the lower bunk's metal frame, ready to hoist herself up to the upper bed.

The massive man's hand shot out, grabbing her ankle. His grip was like iron, fingers digging into her flesh.

"New meat doesn't climb without permission," he growled in Russian, his voice a deep rumble that seemed to vibrate through the cell's concrete walls. His eyes remained closed, face impassive, as if restraining her required no more attention than swatting a fly.

Anna froze. Not from fear, but calculation. The grip was a test. React too aggressively, and she'd make an enemy on her first night. Show too much weakness, and she'd be marked as prey.

"My apologies," she replied in Russian, her voice deliberately pitched lower than her natural tone. "I didn't wish to disturb your rest."

The man opened one eye, studying her with unexpected shrewdness. "American," he observed, his grip still firm around her ankle. "What's an American doing in Astrakhan Central?"

"Making poor life choices," Anna replied, the dry humor delivered in a flat tone.

The corner of the man's mouth twitched—not quite a smile, but recognition of her attempt at prison diplomacy. His grip loosened slightly.

"I am Vadim," he said. "This is my cell. You sleep where I say you sleep."

Anna nodded once, acknowledging his authority without challenging it. Prison hierarchy was simple on the surface, complex in its execution. She needed to navigate it carefully until she located her target.

From the single bunk across the cell, the second man spoke without opening his eyes or changing his position.

"Let the American take the top bunk, Vadim," he said in flawless Russian, his voice surprisingly soft and cultured. "He's too skinny to be worth your attention."

Vadim's hand released Anna's ankle. "You're lucky Nikolai speaks for you," he rumbled, settling back into his bunk. "Tomorrow, we decide if you belong here."

Anna climbed to the upper bunk without further comment. The thin mattress crackled beneath her weight—plastic-covered foam, designed to be easily cleaned and resistant to concealment. A single blanket lay folded at the foot of the bunk, gray and thin from countless washings.

She lay on her back, staring at the ceiling barely a foot above her face. The concrete was etched with the markings of previous occupants—tallies of days, crude drawings, names scratched into the surface with whatever sharp objects could be smuggled past the guards. In the dim light, these inscriptions looked like ancient cave paintings, a primitive record of human suffering.

Anna regulated her breathing, ignoring the discomfort. Her mind mapped the cell block from what she had observed during her entry: guard rotations, camera placements, blind spots. All of this added up to a pulse... the prison's rhythm. Every facility had one—like a heartbeat, regular and predictable once you learned to feel it.

She had almost slipped into a light meditative state when footsteps approached—deliberate, unhurried. The sound of a baton dragging along the cell bars created a metallic symphony that grew louder as the source drew near. The block guard was making rounds.

The footsteps stopped outside their cell. Anna sensed the presence more than saw it—a shadow blocking the already minimal light from the corridor. The baton tapped against the bars once, twice, three times. A summons, not a warning.

Anna remained still, feigning sleep. The tapping continued, more insistent.

"American," a voice called softly. "I know you're awake. Come here."

She opened her eyes slowly, turning her head toward the voice. The block guard stood outside the cell, his face half-illuminated by the corridor's dim lighting. His eyes tracked her movements as she silently swung her legs over the edge of the bunk and dropped to the floor with barely a sound.

Vadim's breathing changed subtly—he was awake, listening, but choosing not to interfere. Across the cell, Nikolai remained motionless, but Anna sensed his awareness, the slight tension in his shoulders betraying his consciousness.

She approached the bars, stopping just out of arm's reach. The guard's eyes traveled over her face, lingering on her features in a way that sent warning signals through her mind. His gaze was evaluative, intrusive—predatory.

"You're pretty," he said in Russian, his voice low enough not to carry beyond their immediate vicinity, "for a man." The guard's tongue darted out to wet his lips, a gesture both unconscious and revealing. "Too pretty for Cell Block D."

Anna didn't speak, didn't react. Her face remained impassive, even as her mind measured new threats, new variables. The guard's interest was dangerous—not just for her cover, but for the mission. Unwanted attention from any quarter increased risk exponentially.

The guard leaned closer, his breath fogging the metal bars between them. It smelled of cigarettes and cheap alcohol, sour and stale. His face hovered in the dim corridor light—pockmarked skin stretched over sharp cheekbones, a thin mustache above cracked lips. His eyes were a faint blue, almost colorless in the shadows with yellowed whites that spoke of decades of hard living.

"They say you killed a man," he whispered, fingers wrapping around the bars. The knuckles were scarred, misshapen from past violence. A crude tattoo of a dagger stretched across the back of his right hand, its tip pointing toward his wrist. "Tortured him first. Is that true, pretty boy?"

Anna maintained her silence, her green eyes reflecting nothing back to him. Behind her, she sensed Vadim shifting slightly on his bunk, the metal frame creaking under his massive weight.

The guard's expression darkened at her silence. A vein throbbed visibly at his temple.

"I asked you a question," he hissed, tapping his baton against the bars with increasing force. Each impact sent metallic vibrations through the cell. "When I ask, you answer. That's how things work here."

Anna remained still, her face a mask of indifference. The guard represented a complication—one that could derail everything if not handled properly. But engaging him now, in any way, would establish a dynamic she couldn't afford.

"You think you're tough?" The guard's voice rose slightly, color flooding his blanched cheeks. "I've broken men twice your size. By the time I'm done with you, you'll be begging to answer my questions."

His fingers tightened around the bars until the knuckles turned white. The corridor light caught the sheen of sweat on his forehead, the dilated pupils that suggested more than just alcohol in his system. The night shift often brought out the worst in those already inclined toward darkness.

"Maybe you need some time in the special room," he continued, voice dropping to a whisper again. "No cameras there. Just you and me and a conversation about respect."

From the opposite bunk, Nikolai's voice drifted through the darkness. "The American is under *vor* protection, Yegor." His tone was casual, conversational, but carried an unmistakable warning. "Vadim has claimed him."

The guard's eyes flicked toward Nikolai, then to Vadim's massive form. Something passed across his face—the recognition of boundaries even he wouldn't cross. The thieves-in-law held their own form of authority within the prison walls, one that even guards respected—or feared.

"Is that so?" The guard—Yegor—spat on the concrete floor outside the cell, taking a moment to absorb the thought, weighing it for authenticity.

Anna did the same, though her expression was much more subtle, a schooled neutrality that gave away nothing. Yes, for some reason, she had been claimed and protected... but how well? Would much effort be put into avenging her—a stranger, no matter how respectful—if something happened while Nikolai and Vadim were not present?

A face of false affability fell over Yegor's expression like a mask. "My apologies then. It seems you are good at making friends, American." His pale eyes fixed on Anna again. "Until our next meeting."

With that, he tapped his baton against the bars one final time and continued his rounds, footsteps fading into the ambient noise of the sleeping cell block.

Anna remained standing by the bars for several moments, her face revealing nothing of her mind. This guard was a complication—unpredictable, unstable, and now fixated on her. She filed the information away, another variable to manage in an already complex equation.

"You should thank me," Nikolai said softly from his bunk, still not moving from his position. "Yegor enjoys breaking new arrivals—especially the ones who don't fit the usual mold."

Anna turned slowly, facing her cellmate across the narrow space. "Thank you," she said, her voice measured, accent carefully maintained.

Vadim sat up on his bunk, the metal frame groaning beneath his weight. In the dim light, his tattoos seemed to shift and move across his skin like living things. "Sit," he commanded, patting the edge of his mattress.

It wasn't a request. Anna moved to the indicated spot, perching on the edge of Vadim's bunk, maintaining a calculated distance—close enough to show respect, far enough to react if necessary.

"You have strange tattoos," Vadim observed, his eyes roaming over Anna's exposed forearms where her sleeves had been rolled up. "Strange for a killer."

"I prefer discretion," Anna replied.

Vadim's laugh was like distant thunder. "In prison, there is no discretion. Only survival." He leaned closer, his massive bulk casting her in shadow. "What did the man do to deserve torture before death?"

Anna met his gaze directly. "He pretended to be someone he wasn't."

Something flickered in Vadim's eyes—recognition, perhaps, or appreciation for the layers of meaning. Across the cell, Nikolai shifted slightly, turning to face them. In the shadows, his eyes gleamed with intelligence and appraisal.

"And who are you?" Nikolai asked, his voice soft but penetrating. "Besides American?"

"Nobody," Anna replied. "Just someone passing through."

Vadim's hand shot out, grabbing Anna's jaw. His fingers dug into her skin as he turned her face from side to side, examining her features in the dim light. The grip was painful, but Anna showed no reaction, her green eyes remaining steady and unblinking.

"Not nobody," Vadim said, relaxing that iron grip as suddenly as he had grabbed her—but not removing his hand. "Something in the eyes. A wolf among dogs." He nodded, as if confirming something to himself. "You may have the top bunk. But tomorrow, you will tell us why you are really here. The *vor's* protection is not unconditional."

She exhaled slowly. Too far. She drew the line at manhandling. "Let go of me."

The man stared at her. She spoke calmly, cold, her voice like ice.

Vadim's eyes widened slightly, his massive body tensing. For a moment, the cell seemed to shrink, the air between them charged with potential violence. Anna didn't flinch, didn't blink, didn't break eye contact.

Across the cell, Nikolai sat up slowly, his movements fluid and silent. "Interesting," he murmured, almost to himself.

Vadim's face darkened, veins standing out on his thick neck. Then, unexpectedly, his expression shifted. A smile spread across his face, revealing teeth stained from years of prison cigarettes and poor dental care.

"The American has fangs," he rumbled, voice laced with something like respect as he released his fingers. "Good. The weak don't survive here."

He leaned back, massive shoulders resting against the concrete wall. "Sleep while you can," he advised, still studying Anna with new interest. "Morning comes early in Astrakhan Central."

Anna returned to her bunk without another word, climbing up with economical movements. She lay on her back, staring at the ceiling, listening to the prison's nocturnal soundtrack—distant shouts, the occasional clang of metal against metal, the soft moans of men trapped in nightmares they couldn't escape.

Vadim's breathing eventually deepened into sleep. Across the cell, Nikolai remained awake, his presence felt rather than heard. Anna sensed his attention, his evaluation continuing in the darkness.

"Whatever you're looking for," Nikolai whispered finally, his voice barely audible above the ambient noise, "I hope it's worth dying for."

Anna didn't respond. The mission was always worth dying for. That had been drilled into her from the beginning. The objective above all else. Personal survival was secondary.

But as she lay in the darkness of cell 217, surrounded by concrete and steel and men who killed as easily as they breathed, Anna found herself thinking not of the mission but of Beth. Her sister's face floated in her mind—smiling, trusting, unaware of the shadows Anna kept at bay.

If she failed here, those shadows would find Beth. The Albino would make sure of it. The thought hardened something inside her, a resolve that went beyond training, beyond duty.

She'd come here for a reason.

The Albino might've hidden himself behind these walls, but they called her the Guardian Angel.

Angels, like ghosts, weren't stopped by walls.

Chapter 6

Anna knew trouble was coming in the meal hall after only a few minutes. Too pretty. That's what the guard had said, and that's what other inmates were now likely whispering to each other as they watched her move along the meal line.

It didn't matter too much what the prisoners thought, not for a while, at least. People kept their thoughts to themselves if you had their respect. And respect in a place like this was earned.

She moved calmly through the meal line, alone—isolated. She often felt alone. She operated best alone. And as she did, three men were sitting at a table near the chow line, eyeing her like wolves examining a slab of meat.

Anna felt the eyes tracking her as she moved through the meal line—casual observation disguised as disinterest. Professional assessment masked itself as idle curiosity, but she saw through the side-eyed looks. These weren't ordinary glances—they were appraisals of weakness, evaluations of potential resistance, measurements of worth.

The dining hall of Astrakhan Central Prison operated according to unwritten rules more rigid than any formal code. Tables were claimed territories. Seating arrangements reflected alliances, ethnicity, criminal affiliations. The acoustics were deliberately poor—a cacophony of clattering trays, scraping chairs, and overlapping conversations that made surveillance difficult. Perfect for whispered threats, for deals made beyond official hearing.

Anna accepted a metal tray from a trustee with downcast eyes. The food was predictably grim—gray porridge with the consistency of wet cement, black bread dense enough to use as a weapon, tea that resembled dirty dishwater. It was calories, not cuisine. Fuel for bodies so the facility could continue to maintain their charges without providing satisfaction for their appetites.

Moving further in, Anna scanned the room without seeming to, cataloging threats and opportunities with practiced efficiency.

The three men at the table near the serving line represented the most immediate concern. Their posture, their positioning, the way they tracked her movements—it was all classic predatory behavior. They'd marked her as a target. The question was whether this was a test, a territorial display, or something more personal.

Vadim sat with a group of tattooed men at a table in the center of the hall—prime real estate in prison geography. The thieves-in-law operated as a society within a society, with their own hierarchy, their own justice. Vadim's position at the center of the table, with men flanking him like courtiers around a king, confirmed what Anna had already suspected. He wasn't just any prisoner. He was authority.

Nikolai was nowhere to be seen. Anna made a mental note of his absence. In prison, patterns mattered. Disruptions to routine signaled potential problems.

They had said flooding had affected solitary.

Flooding meant crews to clean—to fix, to paint.

She needed access. And a cleaning crew position might just be her ticket.

Moving away from the serving line, tray balanced in her hands, face carefully blank, Anna noted the change in the three men watching her. One nodded slightly, exchanging a glance with the others. Another shifted in his seat, hand dropping below the table—a classic preparation for violence.

Anna had options. She could seek Vadim's protection, sitting at or near his table—a declaration of allegiance that would come with expectations and obligations she couldn't afford to provide or ignore. She could find an empty table, projecting isolation and self-sufficiency—a stance that would mark her as either weak or challenging, depending on how she carried it. Or she could address the threat directly, eliminating the ambiguity.

She chose the third option.

With deliberate steps, Anna approached the table where the three men sat. Their conversations stopped as she drew near; the one with his hand below the table—a large man, barrel-chested and scarred in a way that drew his lip into a permanent sneer—hesitated and looked to the others as if seeking instruction. The smallest man—wiry, with nervous energy that manifested in constantly moving fingers—smiled, revealing teeth filed to points. The third man, seated with his back to the wall, watched her approach with cold assessment in his eyes. Unlike his companions, he remained perfectly still, only his gaze tracking her movement—a spider waiting in its web.

Anna stopped before their table, tray held steady in her hands. The dining hall's ambient noise seemed to dim as nearby conversations faltered, attention shifting to the unfolding scene.

"You're in my seat," she said in Russian, her voice pitched low but carrying clearly to the men before her.

The scarred man blinked, momentarily thrown by her directness. Then his face darkened, blood rushing to his cheeks in mottled patches.

"What did you say, pretty boy?" he growled, massive hands flattening on the table's surface.

"I said," Anna repeated, her tone unchanged, "you're in my seat."

The man with filed teeth giggled, a high-pitched sound incongruous with the prison setting as he addressed his larger friend. "Is he crazy, Volkov? I think he's crazy."

The third man—the one with calculating eyes—studied Anna more intently now. "American," he observed quietly. "New arrival. Cell Block D." His Russian was precise, academic. "There are no assigned seats in the dining hall."

"There are now," Anna replied.

At the surrounding tables, conversations had stopped entirely. A slow ripple of tension radiated out until even the trustees behind the serving line had faltered in their duties, ladles suspended over steaming trays. At the central table, Vadim watched with undisguised interest, massive arms folded across his chest.

The scarred man—Volkov—stood slowly, unfolding to his full height. He towered over Anna by at least twenty centimeters, his shoulders broad enough to cast her in shadow. Prison muscle, built from years of nothing to do but lift makeshift weights in the yard.

"You want to die on your first day?" Volkov asked, voice rumbling from deep in his chest. "Is that it?"

Anna set her tray down on the table with careful precision. "I want to establish clarity," she said. "So there are no misunderstandings moving forward."

The man with filed teeth rose as well, circling around the table like a hyena approaching wounded prey. The third man remained seated, his expression neutral but attentive. His stillness was more concerning than his companions' overt aggression.

Guards stationed along the dining hall's perimeter watched with professional disinterest. Prison violence followed its own ecosystem. Unless it threatened overall order, they rarely intervened.

"Clarity," Volkov repeated, the word clumsy in his mouth. "I'll give you clarity." His hand moved to his waistband, where the outline of something thin and rigid pressed against the fabric of his prison uniform.

GUARDIAN'S MISSION

Anna moved.

Her right hand shot forward, fingers driving into Volkov's throat with surgical precision—not enough force to crush his windpipe, but sufficient to collapse it temporarily. As he gasped, hands flying to his neck, she pivoted smoothly, using his momentum to guide him face-first onto the table. His forehead connected with the metal surface with a hollow thunk that echoed through the suddenly silent dining hall.

The man with filed teeth lunged, a sharpened toothbrush handle emerging from his sleeve. Anna sidestepped, her left hand catching his wrist, twisting sharply. Bone snapped with an audible crack. The weapon clattered to the floor as he howled, dropping to his knees.

The third man—the calculating one—hadn't moved from his seat. His lightly tinted eyes tracked every motion, assessing, learning. This, Anna recognized, was the true threat. Not the muscle or the madness, but the mind that directed them.

Volkov recovered enough to swing a massive fist toward her head. Anna ducked beneath it, stepping inside his reach. Her elbow connected with his floating rib—another precise strike, enough to disable without permanent damage. Volkov doubled over, air rushing from his lungs.

The entire sequence had taken less than six seconds.

Anna straightened, adjusting her prison uniform with small, economical movements. The dining hall remained silent, every eye fixed on the scene. Guards had finally started moving toward the disturbance, batons drawn.

"As I said," Anna addressed the third man, who still hadn't risen from his seat, "clarity."

The man nodded once, a gesture of acknowledgment rather than submission. "Impressive," he said quietly. "But unwise."

Before Anna could respond, guards surrounded them, batons raised. "On the ground!" one shouted. "All of you!"

Anna complied immediately, kneeling with her hands behind her head. Volkov remained doubled over, struggling to breathe. The man with the broken wrist continued to whimper, cradling his injured arm. Only the third man moved with the same calm deliberation as Anna, placing his hands on his head as he knelt beside the table.

"You." A guard pointed his baton at Anna, "Your cell *now*!"

Her cell—not to isolation then.

Her eyes narrowed. As she suspected, there was more to this embargo on isolation than just a flood fix. Was the Albino intentionally keeping people away from his inner sanctum?

GUARDIAN'S MISSION

That seemed likely.

As two guards gripped her arms to pull her up, Anna caught Vadim's gaze across the dining hall. The *vor's* expression was unreadable, but he inclined his head slightly—acknowledgment, perhaps, or something more. Beside him, a space had opened up at the table, as if someone had vacated their seat in a hurry.

The guards marched Anna from the dining hall, her arms twisted behind her back in a control hold. She didn't resist. This, too, had been calculated—a controlled introduction to the prison population, followed by strategic removal.

The guards escorted Anna back to her cell, their grip unnecessarily tight on her arms. Her mind was already mapping the consequences of her display in the dining hall—the alliances shifting, the readjustments being made by those who had witnessed her efficiency—changing their view of the ecosystem to account for her. Violence in prison was currency, but precision violence was capital.

"You've got a death wish," one guard muttered as they marched her through the corridors. "Nobody touches Volkov's crew. Nobody."

Anna remained silent. The guard's warning was information, nothing more. Volkov wasn't her concern. The Albino was.

Everything else was noise, distraction, environmental factors to be managed.

They reached cell 217 and he shoved her inside with more force than necessary. The door slid shut with a metallic clang that echoed through the block.

"Enjoy your last night breathing," the guard called through the bars before walking away, keys jangling at his belt.

Anna stood motionless in the center of the cell, listening as the guard's footsteps faded. The cell block was nearly empty, most prisoners still at the dining hall. She had perhaps fifteen minutes before they returned—fifteen minutes to process, plan, adapt.

"Impressive performance."

The voice came from the shadows in the corner of the cell. Nikolai sat on his bunk, legs crossed, watching her with those examining eyes. He must have skipped the meal entirely, remaining behind when the others left.

"You saw?" Anna asked, moving to her bunk.

"No," Nikolai replied. "But word travels fast, even in these walls. Especially in these walls." He tilted his head slightly. "You disabled three men in seconds. Efficiently. Professionally. Without killing them."

GUARDIAN'S MISSION

He had a phone, she realized. Someone had either sent him a video or made a call. Perhaps the man missing from the seat next to their other roommate.

Anna climbed to her bunk, settling against the wall, face betraying nothing.

"Military," Nikolai continued, as if thinking aloud. "Special forces, perhaps. American accent, but fluent Russian. Not CIA—they have better covers. Private contractor, maybe, but you lack the mercenary mentality." His eyes narrowed slightly. "You fight like someone trained to neutralize, not eliminate. Precise. Controlled. You could have killed them all but chose not to."

"Is there a question in there?" Anna asked.

Nikolai's smile was small but genuine. "Many. But the most pressing is: why are you really here, in a Russian prison, deliberately drawing attention to yourself?"

Anna just shrugged.

"Those tattoos... I asked."

He was gesturing at the bone-frog and the trident visible on her forearms.

The man gestured at the tattoos on Anna's forearms—simple designs that could be read multiple ways. "American special forces symbols," Nikolai observed quietly. "Yet your file says you're a civilian with no military background."

Anna remained silent. He had access to her file and to a phone—more useful information.

"You know," Nikolai continued when she didn't respond, "Vadim is impressed. He doesn't impress easily." His eyes never left her face, studying every microexpression. "He's decided you're worth protecting."

"I didn't ask for his protection," Anna replied, voice neutral.

"No one asks for it. They earn it." Nikolai uncrossed his legs, leaning forward slightly. "What you did in the dining hall—that earned you something. Respect, perhaps. Or at least curiosity. You have his attention and have proven you might be a useful tool to him. This is a *good* impression to cultivate."

The distant sound of voices grew louder—prisoners returning from the meal. Anna estimated she had maybe two minutes before the cell block filled again.

"Volkov's crew will come for you," Nikolai said matter-of-factly. "Not today. Maybe not tomorrow. But they will come. And when they do, they'll bring numbers."

"I'm aware."

"Are you also aware that the man you didn't engage—the one who stayed seated—is Anton Barkov?" Nikolai's voice dropped lower. "Former GRU intelligence officer. Disgraced, imprisoned, but still connected. He doesn't forget faces."

That was a complication. GRU meant military intelligence: connections, resources—a man who could potentially recognize her or trace her background if he became too curious.

The voices grew louder. Footsteps echoed on metal stairs.

"Whoever you're hunting in here," Nikolai said, eyes glinting in the dim light, "I hope they're worth the attention you've drawn."

"I never said I was hunting anyone. But what I want to know is the price."

"Hmm?"

"What price are you asking for protection?"

He smiled at her, a shark's smile.

"A favor," he said simply.

"What favor is that?"

He didn't answer right away, it seemed he too considered his words carefully.

Nikolai's eyes seemed to change in the dim light—shifting from mechanical to something deeper, almost contemplative. He leaned back against the concrete wall, his movements fluid and economical, like those of a dancer or an assassin. The ambient sounds of the prison—the returning prisoners, the metallic clangs of doors, the distant shouts—all seemed to fade as he considered her question.

"The favor," he began, his voice pitched just loud enough for Anna to hear but no further, "is information. For now."

Anna said nothing, waiting. In prison, as in intelligence work, patience often revealed more than questions.

"You're observant," Nikolai continued, his fingers tracing an invisible pattern on his knee. "I need to know what you see. Who comes, who goes. Which guards speak to which prisoners. The rhythm of this place. You'll be my eyes in places I cannot be."

It was reasonable enough on the surface—a common prison arrangement. Information was currency behind bars, sometimes more valuable than cigarettes or violence even. But Anna sensed layers beneath the request, complexities hidden behind the simplicity.

"And in exchange?" she asked.

"In exchange, I offer knowledge." Nikolai's lips curved into a smile that didn't reach his eyes. "About the isolation wing. About who receives special treatment there. About the hidden places in this prison where certain... individuals are kept away from the general population."

Anna's interest sharpened, though she kept her face carefully neutral. This was potentially useful—directly relevant to her search for the Albino.

"The isolation wing is currently closed for repairs," she noted, testing him.

Nikolai's smile widened fractionally. "So they say. Convenient timing, wouldn't you agree? Just as certain new prisoners arrive, just as certain guards are rotated to different shifts." His voice dropped even lower. "Just as the warden begins receiving visitors at unusual hours."

Outside their cell, shadows moved as prisoners returned to their bunks. Voices echoed off concrete and steel. The cell block was filling again.

Looking out for Vadim, Anna felt a faint disruption in the pattern. Where was the bull-shouldered *vor*?

"If you're looking for our friend, he will be late returning," Nikolai said with a smirk. "You caused a fuss in the dining hall and Vadim is your cell mate. Being a man of influence in here, they are likely trying to ply him with real food, cigars, or perhaps women to discover who you are. Do not be troubled, though. Vadim knows better than most how to navigate those 'private conversations'. One does not last long in here once they acquire the reputation of a rat."

"You've been here a long time," Anna observed.

"Long enough to recognize patterns. Long enough to see the corruption seeping through these walls like the damp." Nikolai's gaze drifted to the ceiling, where water stains created abstract patterns on the concrete. "Long enough to understand that Astrakhan Central isn't just a prison. It's a business. An enterprise."

"Bullshit," she finally said.

He blinked.

"What do you really want? Don't lie to me. I don't do well with liars."

Nikolai frowned briefly. Perhaps he wasn't used to someone he couldn't scare. He studied her. "You don't look like a man."

She shrugged. "I've killed enough."

He smirked. "That is what I want."

She waited.

"Something you seem suited to, no?"

"You want me to kill someone?"

He frowned at how she said it, loud and brazen. He licked his lips nervously, glancing over her shoulder, through the bars.

He was scared.

Nikolai leaned forward, his voice dropping to a whisper so faint Anna had to strain to hear it, even in the confines of their small cell.

"The warden," he breathed, the words barely disturbing the air between them. "I want you to kill the warden."

Anna's expression remained impassive, but her mind rapidly assessed this new information. A significant request—far beyond the standard prison politics she'd anticipated.

Nikolai's eyes darted toward the cell door again, checking for listeners. When he continued, his voice was a thread of sound that seemed to dissolve into the ambient noise of the prison.

"Warden Sokolov isn't just corrupt," he said. "He's a monster wearing human skin."

Anna said nothing, waiting. Prison was full of monsters, both real and imagined. Claims required verification.

"Three weeks ago," Nikolai continued, "a prisoner was taken to his office. Nineteen years old. First offense. Nonviolent—well, as gentle as it can be to end up here. He was pretty. Pretty, like you." His fingers twitched slightly against his leg, the only sign of emotion. "The boy was returned to his cell the next morning. Couldn't speak. Wouldn't eat. Hung himself with his bedsheet two days later."

He paused, gauging Anna's reaction. Finding none, he pressed on.

"Last month, a woman guard who threatened to report certain... irregularities... was found in the prison parking lot. Official report says she crashed her car. Witnesses say the brake lines were cut. The investigation disappeared as quickly as she did."

Anna remained still, cataloging the information without judgment. Nikolai's hatred seemed genuine, but hatred alone wasn't evidence.

"The isolation wing," he said, voice hardening slightly. "That's where he conducts his business. Not just prison business. The other kind. The kind that leaves bodies floating in the Volga. The kind that ships young women to Turkey in containers.

The kind that moves things through the port that shouldn't be moved."

A muscle in Nikolai's jaw tightened. "The flooding is convenient, yes? No access. No witnesses. Just Sokolov and his special guards and whoever pays enough to use his facilities."

Anna's interest sharpened. If the warden was running operations from the isolation wing, it could explain why the Albino had chosen Astrakhan Central as his hiding place. There wasn't just prison protection here but business opportunities, infrastructure... connections.

"You have access to a phone," she observed quietly. "You have information about my file. You're not an ordinary prisoner."

Nikolai's smile was cold. "And you're not an ordinary killer. We all wear masks in here, some better than others."

The cell block had grown quieter as prisoners settled into their bunks. The overhead lights dimmed slightly—the prison's signal that free movement time was ending. Soon the night lockdown would begin.

"Why do you care?" Anna said quietly. "About the warden?" She kept her voice low, rasping. It was beginning to hurt.

Nikolai's face changed subtly in the half-light. Something flashed across his features—a ripple of emotion quickly suppressed, like a stone dropped into still water. His eyes, normally calculating and cold, briefly held something Anna recognized immediately: raw pain.

He turned his face away, gaze fixed on a point on the wall where the concrete had chipped away, revealing older layers beneath. His fingers—long, elegant, incongruous in this place of brutality—traced invisible patterns on his knee. The silence between them expanded, filled with the ambient sounds of the prison at night: distant coughs, the occasional shout, the metallic groans of an aging building settling into darkness.

When he finally spoke, his voice had changed. The academic precision remained, but beneath it lay something jagged and unhealed.

"There are things even these walls won't contain," he said, so quietly Anna had to strain to hear. "Memories. Nightmares. The faces of those who didn't survive."

A guard passed by their cell, flashlight beam sweeping across the floor, briefly illuminating Nikolai's profile. His features looked carved from stone, the shadows emphasizing the hollows beneath his cheekbones, the slight asymmetry of a nose that had been broken and reset.

"Sokolov has run this prison for seven years," he continued once the guard had passed. "Before that, he was FSB. Before that..."

His hand made a dismissive gesture. "Before that doesn't matter. What matters is what he's built here: a kingdom of suffering, an enterprise fueled by blood."

Anna watched him carefully. This wasn't just professional hatred or prison politics. This was personal—deeply, viscerally personal. She recognized the quality of his restraint, the careful containment of something that, if released, would consume everything in its path. She'd felt it herself, directed it, used it as fuel when nothing else remained.

Nikolai's eyes found hers again, searching for something—understanding, perhaps, or the recognition of a shared darkness.

"How do I get into isolation?" Anna asked, cutting through the emotion with practical necessity.

Nikolai blinked, momentarily thrown by her directness. Then he shook his head, a small, tight movement. "Not possible. Not now. The flooding is real enough—Sokolov arranged it himself. Water damage to the electrical systems. Convenient."

"Then how do I get someone out of isolation?" The question was direct, almost blunt in the hushed atmosphere they'd created.

Nikolai hesitated, studying her face as if seeing it for the first time. A slow smile spread across his features—not warm, but appreciative, like a chess player recognizing a worthy opponent's strategy.

"For that," he said softly, "I may have an idea." His eyes narrowed slightly. "But do you agree to my terms?"

Anna considered the terms. The warden was a complication, possibly an obstacle between her and the Albino. If Nikolai's assessment was accurate, Sokolov was more than corrupt—he was running operations that likely entangled with her target's activities. Eliminating him might create chaos, an opportunity to access restricted areas during the confusion.

She weighed the variables with cold precision. One more death. One more body. The scales of her conscience had long ago ceased to register such small additions to their burden. She had killed for her country, for her mission, for survival. What difference did motive make when the outcome was the same? Death came to all eventually. She merely accelerated the inevitable for selected individuals. And if the warden was an evil man? Perhaps she needed to consider him collateral.

She thought of Beth—of the real target, of the bloody price she'd already paid in this hunt.

The dim light cast half of Nikolai's face in shadow as he waited for her answer. In that moment, with his features partially obscured, he resembled a classical painting of judgment—half in darkness, half in light, weighing souls at the threshold between worlds.

Anna's mind flashed briefly to Beth. To her sister's face, to the life she'd tried to build away from violence. To the reason she hunted the Albino with such relentless focus. Some deaths served a greater purpose. Some eliminated threats to those who deserved protection.

She'd assassinated plenty for the government. She wasn't a tame killer.

She nodded once, a single, decisive movement, and the deal was sealed in the silent language of killers.

Nikolai's expression didn't change, but something in his eyes shifted—a flicker of satisfaction quickly concealed behind his usual coldness. "Good," he whispered, the word barely disturbing the air between them.

She didn't reply.

He'd come to her, a stranger. A test?

No. He was a man: a desperate man... a very, very desperate man. He'd tried before, no doubt. And now, he was scared.

And so he'd taken his last shot.

But she was desperate too. And she wasn't scared.

Not in the least.

"So, now that we have a deal, how do I get someone out of isolation?" she repeated.

He only looked at her and smiled. "First you solve my problem. *Then* I solve yours."

Just then, an alarm started blaring, red lights flashing outside the bars.

Chapter 7

Anna approached the bars, peering over the railing towards the floor below.

Six guards were corralling a single man. His head was shaved, his eyes blazing. A wound bled over one of his eyes—a washed iris, nearly colorless.

Anna blinked, then let out slow exhale that sounded like the hiss of a snake.

"What is it?" Nikolai asked from behind her.

"I recognize that man."

Nikolai joined her at her side. "Who? The one with the crazy eyes?"

The crazy-eyed man didn't seem to notice the blood seeping into his eyes from the wound over his head. He shouted, swinging a fist and sending one of the guards to the ground, out cold.

Nikolai gave a low whistle.

"He tried to kill me last week," Anna murmured. "Twice."

Nikolai glanced at her. "And he's still alive? Impressive. What's his name?"

"You don't know?"

"New detainee. Came in only a few days before you. Something about killing a port authority official."

Anna winced.

"His name?"

"Kovac..." Under her breath, Anna muttered, "He looks worse without his hair."

The last she'd seen him, she'd nearly killed him on the roof top of a Turkmeni palace. He'd been shooting at her.

Anna studied the man below as the guards struggled to contain him. Even shackled and outnumbered, Kovac moved with a lethal grace that betrayed his military background. Each movement was precise, economical, without wasted energy—the hallmark of someone who had turned violence into an art form.

"Kovac," she repeated, the name tasting like copper on her tongue. "Former Spetsnaz. Alpha Group, I think. Though there are rumors he served in even darker corners of Russian special forces."

Below them, Kovac drove his forehead into a guard's face with such force that the sound of breaking bone carried even over the blaring alarms. Blood sprayed in an arc that caught the red emergency lights, transforming into a momentary crimson constellation before spattering across the concrete floor.

"He's bleeding," Nikolai observed, nodding toward the wound over Kovac's eye. "Yet he doesn't seem to notice."

"Pain is just information to him," Anna replied, watching as three guards finally managed to force Kovac to his knees. "He's trained himself to filter it out, to redirect it. I've seen him walk on a broken leg without limping."

Kovac's head turned suddenly, as if sensing their observation. His eyes like frosted glass swept upward, scanning the tiers until they locked onto Anna's position. Recognition flashed across his face, followed by something that might have been a smile on another man. On Kovac, it was more like a skull's grimace, a death rictus that held no warmth, no humanity.

"He sees you," Nikolai murmured.

"Coincidence. If he was here before me... There's no way he would've known I was coming here," Anna replied softly. " But... he has this... hyper-fixation. Once he targets someone, everything else disappears. The world narrows to just him and his prey."

Kovac's eyes remained fixed on her even as the guards forced his head down, securing a heavy collar around his neck. The restraint was connected to chains that ran to his wrists and ankles, a mobile prison designed for transporting the most dangerous inmates.

"What did you do to earn his attention?" Nikolai asked, a new note of respect in his voice.

Anna watched as the guards hauled Kovac to his feet. "I survived our first encounter."

Below, Kovac was still staring at her, his eyes unblinking despite the blood that continued to seep into them. His lips moved, forming words she couldn't hear over the alarms but could read clearly enough: "Soon."

"He's insane," Nikolai said, not a question but an observation.

"Clinically? Probably. But that's not what makes him lethal." Anna's voice had taken on a quality of professional assessment, one killer evaluating another. "He sees death as poetry. Each kill as a verse in his magnum opus. He approaches murder with what he calls 'elegant brutality.'" She let out a low breath, turning to Nikolai as Kovac was dragged away. "If you want anyone to kill your warden, that's your guy."

"The lunatic? No. Working with a man like that is like burning down your house to kill a rat." Nikolai flashed a thin-lipped smile. He patted her on the arm. "You finish the job I gave you, and I'll help you into solitary."

"I agreed to the deal," Anna murmured. "Don't need to remind me." She turned to him, facing away as Kovac's attention returned to the guards attempting to pull him on. "What can you tell me about the warden? How do I access him?"

"Ah... well..." Nikolai cleared his throat and glanced away. "You're going to have to start a riot."

The alarm continued to blare as Anna processed Nikolai's words.

"A riot," she repeated, voice flat.

Nikolai's eyes gleamed in the pulsing red emergency lights. "The only way to force Sokolov out of his sanctuary. He remains isolated, protected. Comes to the main prison only when absolutely necessary." His voice dropped lower, barely audible beneath the alarms. "But protocol demands his presence during major disturbances."

Anna watched as the guards below finally subdued Kovac, dragging his still-struggling form toward the security doors. Her mind calculated variables, assessed risks, mapped contingencies. A riot meant chaos, unpredictable variables, civilian casualties—other prisoners caught in the crossfire.

"Too messy," she concluded. "Too many witnesses."

"Precisely why it's perfect," Nikolai countered. "Confusion. Panic. Violence from multiple sources. Who could say which hand delivered the fatal blow? In a riot, individual actions become part of a collective storm."

The alarms abruptly silenced, plunging the cell block into artificial quiet. The emergency lights continued to pulse, painting the concrete walls in rhythmic washes of crimson. Guards shouted orders below, their voices echoing through the cavernous space as they secured the area where Kovac had fought.

Anna hesitated. "Where does Volkov's crew usually hang out during recreation time?"

"Ah... well... there are a lot of them in the yard. The guards try to keep them separate at meals—different schedules. But outside for an hour, the whole prison population goes out as one."

"How many men in Volkov's gang?"

"Twenty? Thirty?"

She winced. "That's too many."

"What are you planning?"

"You want a riot, don't you?"

"Yes."

"Well... I already have some history with Volkov. Won't take much to ignite that powder keg."

Nikolai turned away from her, approaching his bed again and letting out a long exhale. "I trust your discretion. Do it fast, though. Time is not on our side."

Chapter 8

Anna paced the yard the next day, wincing under the bright sunlight. After fifteen hours in the artificial light of Cell Block D, the sun felt like an assault, its rays piercing through the thin cloud cover with unexpected ferocity. The prison yard was a concrete rectangle surrounded by twenty-foot walls topped with razor wire. Guard towers occupied each corner, their occupants barely visible behind tinted glass. Snipers, Anna knew, with standing orders to shoot to kill if a riot erupted.

The prisoners had spread themselves across the yard according to unwritten territorial agreements. The thieves-in-law, including Vadim, occupied the weightlifting area—a collection of rusted equipment bolted to the concrete. Various ethnic groups claimed their own sections. Lone wolves and outcasts hugged the walls, trying to remain inconspicuous.

She'd given some consideration to the possibility Kovac would be here too. She would have to account for him... only, as she looked around, it seemed the rumors were true. There had been no room in the isolation block for her. But for Kovac? For the mad-dog with the blood of four guards on him before they had him under control enough to move? For him, they'd found room.

Anna laxly wondered how the Albino would take having to share the isolation block. Then again, perhaps *he* had been the one to order Kovac in and the violence was merely a show. The thought was unnerving, but also unimportant in the moment. She had to focus on the task at hand.

Volkov's crew had positioned themselves near the basketball court, though none were playing. They stood in a loose formation, watching Anna's movements with undisguised hostility. The scarred leader's throat still bore bruising from their encounter in the dining hall. Beside him, the man with filed teeth cradled his broken wrist, now splinted with what looked like stolen medical supplies.

Anton Barkov—the former GRU officer—observed from a distance, his eyes interrogating her. Anna noted his position without appearing to. He was the greater threat—the mind behind Volkov's muscle.

Nikolai was nowhere to be seen—possibly by design. Plausible deniability was often the only layer of protection a prisoner could have in a place like this.

Anna continued her measured pacing, a predator establishing a territory. Her shaved head gleamed in the sunlight, emphasizing the sharp angles of her face. Without hair to soften her features, she looked dangerous—all edges and planes, like a weapon forged rather than born.

The yard hummed with tension. News of yesterday's confrontation had spread through the prison population, creating an atmosphere of anticipation. Violence was entertainment in places like this, a break from the crushing monotony. Prisoners pretended to go about their usual activities while watching for the inevitable clash.

Anna's circuit of the yard brought her closer to Volkov's position. Not directly approaching—that would be too obvious, would give the guards time to intervene—but gradually narrowing the distance. A spiral tightening toward its center.

Across the yard, Vadim watched from his position near the weights. His massive arms were folded across his chest, his expression unreadable. Several of his thieves-in-law brothers flanked him, their tattooed bodies forming a living wall of muscle and criminal authority.

A bell rang—fifteen minutes remaining in the yard period. If Anna was going to act, it needed to be soon. Enough time for chaos to erupt, not enough for guards to fully contain it before the mandatory return to cells.

She changed direction, cutting across the yard at an angle that would bring her within ten meters of Volkov's position. As she moved, she counted guards: six visible on the ground level, four in the towers, likely more waiting in the security stations just inside the yard doors. Standard deployment, but potentially overwhelmed if multiple factions engaged simultaneously.

As Anna drew nearer to Volkov's crew, she noticed Anton Barkov murmuring something to his scarred lieutenant. Volkov's eyes narrowed, his posture shifting subtly from casual hostility to coiled readiness. The man with filed teeth grinned, tongue darting out to lick his pointed incisors in anticipation.

Anna altered her trajectory again, this time angling toward Vadim's territory. The move was deliberate, chosen to create a specific impression: seeking protection. To Volkov's crew, it would look like weakness. To Vadim, like respect for his authority. To the watching prison population, like the next chapter in yesterday's drama.

The yard had grown quieter, conversations tapering off as more eyes turned to watch her movement. Even the basketball game had paused, the ball held forgotten in a player's hands. The prison's collective consciousness sensed the approaching violence like animals before an earthquake.

Anna passed within twenty meters of Vadim's position. She nodded once in his direction—a gesture of acknowledgment, not submission. Vadim returned the nod, massive head dipping almost imperceptibly. The thieves around him shifted, making room as if expecting her to join their circle.

Instead, Anna stopped, turning to face Volkov's approaching crew directly. They had moved to intercept her, spreading out in a loose semicircle to cut off any retreat. Anton Barkov remained slightly behind them, hands clasped behind his back like a general observing troop movements.

"The American thinks he has protection," Volkov called out, his voice carrying across the suddenly silent yard. "Thinks the vor will save him."

Anna didn't respond. Her stance shifted imperceptibly—weight balanced, center of gravity lowered, hands relaxed at her sides. Ready.

"No one touches one of Volkov's men and lives," the scarred man continued, his damaged throat giving his voice a raspy quality. "Not even under vor protection."

From behind Anna, Vadim's voice rumbled like distant thunder. "The American handled himself well yesterday. Perhaps you should reconsider, Volkov."

The yard's tension ratcheted higher. This was no longer just about a new prisoner who had embarrassed Volkov's crew. Now it involved the thieves-in-law, their code, their authority. The prison population watched with collective held breath as invisible lines of power and respect were tested, stretched, threatened.

Volkov spat on the concrete. "The vor are not what they once were," he said, loud enough for all to hear. "Soft. Taking outsiders under their protection. Forgetting the old ways."

A murmur rippled through the yard. This was a direct challenge to Vadim's authority, to the thieves' code itself. The massive vor stepped forward, his face darkening like a gathering storm.

Posturing. It would *all* be posturing... Unless Anna ignited the powder keg she'd created.

And the best way to do that?

To go after the quiet, watching man. Not one of the mercenaries, but to hurt the leader himself.

Six men stood between her and Anton Barkov—the true target. Six obstacles to remove with maximum efficiency and impact. Anna's gaze locked onto Barkov's pale eyes, ignoring Volkov completely. It was a calculated insult—dismissing the muscle to focus on the mind.

"You," she said, addressing Barkov directly. "Former GRU. You should know better than to waste assets on wounded pride."

Barkov's expression didn't change, but something flickered in his eyes—surprise, perhaps, at being singled out. Being recognized. The yard had gone completely silent now, even the guards watching with wary attention, hands on their batons but not yet intervening.

"Assets?" Barkov replied, his academic Russian a stark contrast to Volkov's guttural growl. "An interesting choice of words. Professional terminology."

Volkov glanced between them, momentarily confused by the shift in focus. The delay was all Anna needed.

She moved.

Not toward Volkov as expected, but directly at his lieutenant—the man standing closest to Barkov. Her first strike caught him beneath the sternum, driving upward with enough force to collapse his diaphragm. As he doubled over, gasping for air that wouldn't come, she used his descending momentum to launch herself forward, vaulting over his back toward the next man in line.

The second opponent managed to swing a wild punch that Anna deflected with her forearm, redirecting his energy while simultaneously driving her knee into his groin. He crumpled with a high-pitched wheeze that cut through the shocked silence of the yard.

Two down in less than three seconds.

Volkov bellowed, charging forward like an enraged bull. Anna sidestepped, using his momentum against him, adding a precise strike to his already-damaged throat that sent him staggering into his own men. They collided in a tangle of limbs, momentarily disorganized.

The man with filed teeth lunged next, his good hand clutching a makeshift shiv fashioned from what looked like a sharpened plastic spoon handle. Anna caught his wrist, twisted sharply, and drove her elbow into his temple with controlled force. His eyes rolled back as he collapsed to the concrete.

Three down. The remaining crew members hesitated, suddenly uncertain. This wasn't the fight they had expected. This wasn't a fight at all—it was a systematic dismantling.

Anna continued her advance toward Barkov, who remained motionless, observing with clinical detachment even as his protection crumbled. His lack of fear was notable. Professional. He recognized another predator.

Guards were moving now, blowing whistles, shouting commands, but their voices seemed distant, irrelevant to the focused bubble of violence Anna had created. Prisoners along the yard's perimeter began shouting, some cheering, others joining the growing chaos. The spark was catching, spreading.

"Enough!" Barkov called out, raising a hand to halt his remaining men. Fifteen? Twenty? Some were approaching from other portions of the yard, jogging over, horrified.

But it was too late. The yard had ignited.

Anna saw her opportunity and lunged toward Barkov, closing the distance between them with frightening speed. His eyes widened—not with fear, but with recognition. He moved to counter her, his technique revealing his own training. Former GRU indeed.

Their exchange was brief, precise, a conversation in the language of violence that few in the yard could fully understand. Barkov was good—exceptionally good for a man who had likely spent years behind bars. But Anna was better.

She feinted left, drew his counter, then dropped low and swept his legs from beneath him. As he fell, she drove her knee into his solar plexus, following him to the ground. Their faces were inches apart as she pinned him, her forearm across his throat.

"Who sent you?" he gasped, speaking English now, his accent crisp and educated.

The question caught Anna by surprise—enough that her pressure eased fractionally. Barkov used the moment to buck upward, nearly dislodging her, but she recovered quickly, driving her weight down with renewed force.

Around them, the yard had descended into chaos. Volkov's remaining crew clashed with Vadim's thieves-in-law. Other factions joined the fray, old rivalries erupting in the permission of the moment. Guards shouted, batons swinging, but they were rapidly overwhelmed by the spreading violence.

Two men tried to grab at her, but Vadim's enormous hands grabbed their necks.

She'd anticipated the thieves' reactions accurately. Vadim wouldn't waste the opportunity to expand his power.

This was a man used to control, and she was a tool for him to gain more of it.

"I asked who sent you," Barkov repeated, his ghastly eyes boring into hers with uncanny intensity.

Anna leaned closer, her voice pitched for his ears alone. "No one you know."

His laugh was unexpected—a short, bitter sound. "Everyone I know is either dead or in places like this." His eyes narrowed, studying her face with uncomfortable perception.

A guard appeared through the chaos, baton raised to strike Anna. Without looking, she shifted her weight, catching the descending baton with her free hand while maintaining her position over Barkov. The guard stumbled, off-balance, and Anna used his momentum to pull him forward and down, his head connecting with the concrete beside Barkov's with a sickening crack.

She snatched one of the shivs from Barkov's nearest lieutenant and then, in the chaos, jammed it into the leg of the guard.

The guard screamed. Others began shouting. No gunshots—they didn't want to hit their own.

Barkov snarled, but she punched him in the nose, shattering it. She then knocked him unconscious.

Not much time. The chaos would only continue a bit longer. Smoke was now pouring out over the crowd—tear gas.

She'd anticipated this too. Nikolai had warned her.

The small janitorial door: It was Nikolai's only job—his only assurance. And Anna was about to find out if her new cellmate could be trusted.

Prisoners surged in all directions, some fighting, others seeking shelter from the escalating violence. Guards shouted commands that disappeared into the roar of the riot. Through the spreading tear gas, Anna caught glimpses of batons rising and falling, of bodies colliding, of blood spattering across concrete.

She moved with purpose through the mayhem, using the confusion as cover. Her eyes watered from the gas, but she'd been trained to function through worse. The janitorial door was on the eastern wall—a small maintenance access point that, according to Nikolai, would be unlocked during the confusion.

A guard appeared through the swirling gas, gas mask obscuring his features. Anna dropped low, sweeping his legs from beneath him. As he fell, she stripped the mask from his face and donned it herself, the rubber seal creating a protective barrier against the burning chemicals.

Through the mask's foggy viewplate, she spotted the door—unremarkable, painted the same dull gray as the surrounding wall. A prisoner might pass it a hundred times without noticing. She counted three guards between her position and the target, all occupied with subduing rioters.

Anna moved methodically through the chaos, using other prisoners as shields when necessary. The mask allowed her to see what others couldn't through the thickening gas—pathways, opportunities, threats.

She reached the door, keeping her body close to the wall, shielding her movements from the guard towers. If Nikolai had failed, if the door was locked, her entire plan would collapse. She pressed against the handle.

It gave way.

The door opened inward, revealing a narrow maintenance corridor lit by flickering fluorescents. Anna slipped inside, closing the door behind her. The sounds of the riot immediately dampened, reduced to a distant roar like ocean waves breaking against a shore.

She removed the gas mask, blinking as her eyes adjusted to the dim lighting. The corridor stretched before her, pipes running along the ceiling, the concrete floor stained with decades of industrial cleaning chemicals. It smelled of bleach and mildew, the competing scents creating a uniquely institutional odor.

Nikolai had kept his word. The first test passed.

Anna moved silently down the corridor, following Nikolai's mental map. Three intersections, then right. Past the electrical panels. Through the storage area. Each landmark appeared as predicted, confirming his knowledge of the prison's hidden architecture.

The administrative wing lay beyond the storage area—separated from the prisoner sections by multiple security doors, all of which would normally be locked and monitored. But the riot would have triggered emergency protocols. Security personnel would be deployed to contain the violence, leaving fewer eyes on internal monitors.

She reached the final door—heavier than the others, with a keypad instead of a conventional lock. Nikolai had provided a code: 5-1-4-2-7. Anna hesitated, fingers hovering over the keypad. If he had deceived her, if this was a trap, entering the wrong code would trigger an alarm, bringing guards running.

She punched in the numbers.

The keypad beeped once, a small green light illuminating. The magnetic lock disengaged with a heavy thunk. Anna pushed the door open just enough to slip through, then closed it silently behind her.

She now stood in a carpeted hallway—a stark contrast to the concrete and steel of the prisoner areas. Framed photographs lined the walls: the warden shaking hands with government officials, receiving awards, standing beside uniformed officers.

The carpet muffled her footsteps as she moved past offices with nameplates identifying administrative staff.

At the end of the corridor stood a heavy wooden door with a brass plate: "Warden Sokolov." No keypad here, just a conventional lock. The riot would have brought Sokolov out of isolation, as Nikolai had predicted.

She'd taken the job. Had agreed to deal with the warden.

Nikolai's help had been instrumental.

But now?

If anyone at this prison was protecting the Albino, it sounded like the warden might have a hand in it.

She wasn't here to kill him outright. She needed him. She had one goal, and her mind was fixed on it.

Still, she'd given Nikolai her word in order to gain his aid. The warden, according to Nikolai, was *not* a good man. If he was half of what Nikolai had told her, she would not lose a minute of sleep over his death.

But the others, Casper, Beth, Waldo, had risked too much for her not to fulfill the mission—and that meant she needed him to talk.

Anna reached into her shoe, withdrawing a small, makeshift lockpick created from a metal shiv she'd palmed during the chaos in the yard. The crude tool wasn't ideal, but it would serve. Anna knelt before the lock, inserting the pick with practiced precision.

The lock was quality—not the cheap hardware found in prisoner areas—but Anna had opened far more sophisticated mechanisms under far worse conditions. Her fingers worked delicately, feeling for the pins, applying just enough pressure to set each one without oversetting. The lock surrendered with a soft click that seemed thunderous in the quiet hallway.

She eased the door open and slipped inside, closing it behind her.

The warden's office was opulent compared to the rest of the prison—thick carpet, heavy wooden furniture, walls paneled in dark wood. A large desk dominated the space, its surface organized with military precision. Behind it, floor-to-ceiling windows offered a view of the prison yard, now obscured by tear gas and the chaos of the riot.

The office was empty.

Anna moved quickly to the desk, scanning for information. Computer, phone, papers arranged in neat stacks. A framed photograph showed a younger Sokolov in uniform—special forces insignia visible on his collar. Another displayed him shaking hands with a senior government official Anna recognized from intelligence briefings.

A third frame held a photograph that made Anna pause. Sokolov stood beside a man whose features were familiar from countless intelligence files, countless hours of study, countless nightmares: bloodless skin, colorless eyes, white hair. The Albino.

In the photograph, they were smiling, glasses raised in a toast: comrades... partners.

Anna's suspicions crystallized into certainty. The warden wasn't just protecting the Albino—they were associates, possibly co-conspirators. Nikolai's hatred suddenly made more sense. If Sokolov was working with the Albino, he was complicit in whatever atrocities had earned her target his reputation. Suddenly, she heard footsteps in the corridor outside—heavy, purposeful, nearing rapidly.

Someone was approaching.

Chapter 9

The footsteps advanced toward the warden's door.

Anna's instincts took over. She assessed the office in a fraction of a second—the heavy curtains beside the window, the gap beneath the massive desk, the ornate wooden cabinet in the corner. The footsteps were mere seconds away.

She chose the cabinet, sliding it open to reveal a space just large enough for her slender frame. Inside hung several spare uniforms—the warden's ceremonial attire for official visits and inspections. The wool fabric carried the sharp scent of mothballs and expensive cologne. Anna slipped between the garments, pulling the door nearly closed, leaving only the smallest crack for observation and air.

The office door flew open, banging against the wall with enough force to rattle the framed photographs. Through the narrow gap, Anna watched as Warden Sokolov stormed into the room, followed by two guards and a nervous-looking aide clutching a tablet computer to his chest like a shield.

"Unacceptable!" Sokolov shouted, slamming his fist onto the desk. He was a middle-aged man with a military bearing—broad shoulders, close-cropped silver hair, a face that might have been handsome before years of command had hardened it into perpetual displeasure. His uniform was immaculate despite the chaos erupting elsewhere in the prison, every button gleaming, every crease sharp. "How did this happen?"

The aide flinched, knuckles whitening around his tablet. "Sir, preliminary reports suggest it began with an altercation between Volkov's crew and—"

"I don't care who started it!" Sokolov cut him off, pacing behind his desk like a caged predator. His highly polished boots left indentations in the thick carpet. "We have inspectors arriving tomorrow. Tomorrow! And now I have to explain why my prison erupted into a riot." He turned to the guards—heavy-set men with blank expressions and batons still drawn. "And you two. Where were you when this began? Sleeping? Taking bribes to look the other way?"

The guards exchanged glances but remained silent, their faces betraying nothing. Veteran prison staff, Anna noted, accustomed to being scapegoats for administrative failures. But in that moment, a crumb of unease settled like an itch at the base of Anna's skull... something about them... about that guard on the left...?

Sokolov ran a hand over his face, leaving a smear of sweat across his forehead. Despite his controlled appearance, beads of moisture dotted his hairline, and a slight tremor affected his left hand—signs of stress that his military posture couldn't quite conceal.

"The isolation wing," he said, voice dropping to a harsh whisper. "Is it secure?"

"Yes, sir. Triple guard as ordered. No disturbance there." The taller guard nodded, though Anna's gaze remained on his shorter companion, wishing she could see his face or hear his voice give definition to her unease.

"And our... special guest?" Sokolov asked, glancing nervously at the photograph on his desk.

"Undisturbed, sir," the same guard replied. "As per your standing orders, no one approaches without your direct authorization."

Sokolov's shoulders relaxed marginally, though the tremor in his hand persisted. "Good. That's... good." He turned to his aide. "Contact the regional administrator. Tell him we had a minor disturbance that was quickly contained. No need to postpone tomorrow's inspection."

The aide nodded nervously, fingers dancing across his tablet. "And the injured, sir? Three guards hospitalized. At least twelve prisoners requiring medical attention."

"Exaggerate nothing, minimize everything," Sokolov snapped. "This was a brief altercation between rival factions, nothing more. Routine in a facility of this nature." He straightened his already impeccable jacket. "Now leave me. I need to prepare a statement for the ministry."

The aide scurried from the room, clutching his tablet like a life preserver. The guards turned to follow, but Sokolov held up a hand, stopping the shorter of the two.

"Yegor," he said, his voice dropping to a register that sent a chill through Anna's spine. "Stay a moment."

And there it was. As he'd begun to turn away, Anna caught a glimpse of the shorter guard's pockmarked face and the shadows of the sharp cheekbones flanking his thin mustache.

The shorter guard—Yegor, the same one who had shown interest in Anna at her cell—turned back, standing at attention. "Sir?"

"Close the door."

The taller guard departed, pulling the heavy door shut behind him. The sound of the latch engaging seemed to release something in Sokolov. His military bearing slipped, posture sagging as he dropped heavily into his leather chair.

"Our visitor arrives tonight," he said, voice barely above a whisper. "Everything must be perfect."

Yegor nodded, shifting his weight from one foot to the other. "The isolation wing is prepared, sir. As discussed."

"And the other matter?" Sokolov asked, eyes fixing on Yegor with sudden intensity. "The American?"

Anna froze in her hiding place, hardly daring to breathe.

Yegor's face twisted into something between a smile and a grimace. "Strange one, sir. Doesn't act like the usual prisoners. Too controlled. Too calm."

Sokolov's fingers drummed against his desk, a rapid tattoo that betrayed his inner tension. "I want him taken to interrogation. Questioned. Find out who he really is and why he's here." He opened a drawer, withdrawing a file folder with no markings. "His paperwork is too perfect. Too clean. It stinks of an operation."

"An operation, sir?" Yegor asked, shifting closer to the desk, interest piqued.

"FSB, maybe. Or something worse." Sokolov's voice dropped even lower. "There are rumors from Moscow. Questions being asked about certain shipments—about our arrangement with our special guest."

Yegor's expression darkened. "Should we eliminate the problem?"

Sokolov shook his head, a sharp, decisive movement. "Not yet. Information first." He opened the unmarked folder, revealing photographs that Anna couldn't see from her hiding place. "Find out what he knows, who sent him. Use whatever methods necessary but keep him alive until he talks."

"And after he talks?" Yegor asked, a disturbing eagerness creeping into his voice.

Sokolov closed the folder with a snap. "After he talks, make it look like a prison accident. A fight with another inmate. A suicide. I don't care which, as long as it's convincing." He leaned back in his chair, fingers steepled before him. "Our visitor won't tolerate loose ends, especially now."

Yegor nodded, a thin smile spreading across his face. "I know just how to handle him, sir. The American has already made enemies. Volkov's crew would be happy to assist with his... accident."

"Good. Do it tonight, after the riot is fully contained. Use isolation room three—no cameras there." Sokolov reached for his desk phone. "I need to call our guest. Assure him everything is proceeding as planned despite this... disruption."

From her hiding place, Anna considered her options. Sokolov was clearly protecting the Albino—'our special guest' in isolation. Their arrangement, whatever it entailed, was significant enough to warrant eliminating potential threats. Her cover was compromised, or at least suspected, and time was running out. But who was this *new* guest arriving tomorrow?

A third party?

She decided it didn't matter. She didn't care. Her goal was the Albino.

Yegor gave a small bow and turned to leave.

"One more thing," Sokolov called after him. "The new arrival in isolation. Kovac. Keep him there. Don't let anyone speak to him."

Anna's pulse quickened. So Kovac was in isolation. Interesting. Potentially useful.

Yegor paused at the door. "Understood, sir. Kovac is secured in the high-security section. No contact with anyone."

As the guard left, closing the door behind him, Sokolov reached for his phone. Anna remained motionless in the cabinet, weighing her options. She could attack now—eliminate Sokolov as Nikolai had requested. One swift strike while he was alone and vulnerable. But doing so would sacrifice valuable intelligence about the Albino's location and security.

Sokolov dialed a cell phone, then spoke in a hushed, deferential tone that contrasted sharply with his earlier authority. "Sir, yes. A minor situation, completely contained." He paused, listening. "No, no risk to our arrangement. The shipment will proceed as scheduled." Another pause. "Yes, I understand the importance. All preparations for your arrival are complete."

Anna's mind raced. A shipment. An arrival.

She made up her mind. It wouldn't take long for them to realize she was missing. Anna slipped from the cabinet like a mercury, moving with liquid grace across the thick carpet. Sokolov, still engrossed in his telephone conversation, didn't notice her approach until her shadow fell across his desk. His eyes widened, phone still pressed to his ear, mouth freezing mid-sentence as she closed the distance between them.

Anna struck, her movement so swift it seemed almost casual. The makeshift lockpick shiv flashed in the office's subdued lighting as she pressed it against his carotid artery with just enough pressure to dimple the skin without breaking it.

"Hang up," she commanded, voice low and steady.

Sokolov's finger trembled as he pulled the cell phone from his ear and pressed the button to end the call. His eyes, wide with shock and outrage, fixed on her face, recognition dawning.

"The American prisoner," he breathed, his composure cracking like thin ice. "How did you—"

"Quiet," Anna interrupted, applying slightly more pressure with the shiv. A bead of blood appeared, bright against his ivory skin. "Turn off the phone. Slowly."

He complied, his movements deliberate, controlled despite the fear evident in his quickened breathing. As the smartphone screen flashed its shutdown image, Sokolov's military training was evident—a soldier's discipline reasserting itself even in crisis.

"Whatever you're being paid," Sokolov said, his voice steadier than his hands, "I can double it."

Anna's face remained impassive, her green eyes reflecting nothing back to him. She didn't say a word.

"Then what?" he demanded, a hint of his authority returning. "Information? Revenge? Politics?" His gaze darted to the door, internalizing distances, possibilities.

"The Albino," Anna replied simply.

The effect was immediate and visceral. All color drained from Sokolov's face, his pupils dilating with genuine fear. The name alone had stripped away his veneer of control, revealing the terror beneath.

"You don't understand what you're doing," he whispered, swallowing hard enough that she could see his Adam's apple bob. "He's not someone you can just—"

"Where is he?" Anna cut him off, her voice remaining eerily calm. "Exactly where in the isolation wing?"

Sokolov's expression hardened, a flash of defiance replacing the fear. "I am the warden of this facility. You are a prisoner. This situation ends only one way."

The shiv pressed deeper, drawing a thin line of blood that trickled down his neck, staining his immaculate collar. "You misunderstand. I'm not asking for your cooperation. I'm offering you a choice between information or pain before the inevitable."

His eyes narrowed, military bearing reasserting itself. "You're threatening a government official. The punishment—"

Anna's free hand struck with the precision of a surgeon, fingers driving into a nerve cluster at the junction of his neck and shoulder. Sokolov gasped, his body arching involuntarily as white-hot pain radiated through his nervous system. The technique was designed to cause maximum discomfort without permanent damage—a warning, not a conclusion.

"Let's try again," she said, her voice unnervingly steady. "The Albino. Where?"

Sokolov's face contorted, rage replacing fear as he recovered from the initial shock. His military training reasserted itself, pride overcoming self-preservation.

"You're dead," he snarled, spittle flying from his lips. "You understand? When my men find you, I'll personally oversee your suffering. Days of it. Weeks. You'll beg for death before I'm done with you."

Anna's expression remained impassive, as if he were discussing the weather rather than her torture. The complete absence of fear in her eyes seemed to unnerve him more than any threat could have.

"Your men are busy with a riot," she replied calmly. "And time is something neither of us has in abundance."

Her fingers struck again, this time targeting a different pressure point beneath his jaw. Sokolov's body convulsed, a strangled cry escaping his throat before he could suppress it. Sweat beaded across his forehead, soaking into his silver hair.

"The isolation wing," Anna continued, as if they were having a normal conversation. "Which cell holds the Albino?"

Sokolov's breathing came in ragged gasps. When he could speak again, his voice trembled with fury. "You have no idea what you're dealing with. The Albino isn't just a man. He has connections that reach to the highest levels of government. Touch him, and there's nowhere on earth you can hide."

"I'm not hiding," Anna replied, her green eyes boring into his. "I've been hunting."

Something in her tone—the cold certainty, the predatory focus—finally penetrated Sokolov's armor of authority. His eyes widened slightly as he truly saw her for the first time: not just a prisoner, not just a threat... something else entirely.

"Who are you?" he whispered, a new note of uncertainty in his voice.

Anna didn't answer. Instead, her hand moved with blinding speed, striking a point just below his sternum. The blow was precisely calibrated—enough force to drive the air from his lungs, to create a bubble of pain that would expand through his chest.

Sokolov doubled over as far as the shiv at his throat would allow, face purpling as he struggled to breathe. His hands clutched at the edge of his desk, knuckles whitening as he fought to remain upright.

"I don't care about his connections," Anna said, watching him struggle dispassionately. "And I don't care about your rank. You're taking me to him. Now."

Sokolov's face contorted with pain as he finally drew in a shuddering breath. His eyes, watering from the controlled strike to his solar plexus, fixed on Anna with a mixture of hatred and growing fear.

"You're making a fatal mistake," he wheezed, one hand still pressed against his abdomen. "Even if I told you where he is, you'd never reach him. The isolation wing is a fortress within a fortress."

Anna's expression remained unchanged, the shiv steady against his throat. "Details."

Sokolov laughed—a harsh, bitter sound that ended in a pained cough. Blood from the small nick on his neck had spread across his collar, a crimson stain blooming against the pristine white fabric.

"You want details? Fine." His voice dropped to a rasping whisper. "The isolation wing has three separate security checkpoints. Each requires biometric access—fingerprints, retinal scans, voice recognition. The guards rotate every four hours, with no pattern to their assignments. They're handpicked. Loyal. And they shoot to kill at the first sign of unauthorized access."

He straightened slightly, wincing at the movement. "The corridors between checkpoints are monitored by thermal cameras. Motion sensors trigger lockdown protocols if any movement is detected during red periods. The cell doors themselves require dual authorization—a primary officer and a secondary confirmation from the central security station."

Anna processed this information without reaction, her mind mapping the security measures, identifying weaknesses, calculating possibilities.

"And that's just to reach the regular isolation cells," Sokolov continued, a hint of grim satisfaction creeping into his voice. "The high-security section where the Albino is housed? That's another level entirely. A vault within the vault. Special forces guards. Independent power supply. Panic buttons that trigger flooding protocols if breached."

His eyes gleamed with something like triumph despite his position. "The Albino isn't just any prisoner. He's a valuable asset, protected by people you can't begin to imagine. The security measures around him weren't designed to keep him in—they were designed to keep others out."

Anna's silence seemed to unnerve him. He had expected fear, hesitation, the dawning realization of impossibility. Instead, he faced only that unblinking green gaze, measuring, calculating.

"You still don't understand," Sokolov pressed, his voice taking on an almost desperate quality. "Even if—by some miracle—you managed to bypass every security measure, evade every guard, and reach his cell, what then? The Albino himself is... not normal. The things he's survived, the people he's broken..." He shuddered, a genuine reaction that couldn't be faked. "I've seen hardened killers weep in his presence. Not from pain, but from the weight of his attention."

Sweat trickled down Sokolov's temple as he leaned forward, his voice dropping to a whisper laced with something akin to awe. "You think you're dangerous? You're nothing compared to him. I've seen him kill a man with a look. Just a look. The man's heart simply... stopped."

For the first time, a flicker of emotion crossed Anna's face—not fear, but a cold, terrible anticipation. Her lips curved into the ghost of a smile that didn't reach her eyes.

"Good," she said softly. "I've waited a long time to meet him."

Sokolov stared at her, truly seeing her for perhaps the first time. Whatever he recognized in her expression made him recoil slightly, despite the shiv at his throat.

"You're insane," he whispered.

"No," Anna replied, her voice eerily calm. "I'm focused."

She considered her options. The isolation wing's security as described presented significant challenges. Direct assault was impossible. Stealth approaches were countered by multiple biometric checkpoints. Even with Sokolov as a hostage, she would face overwhelming force before reaching her target.

A different approach was needed, some indirect and unexpected vector.

"I need you to place an order," Anna said abruptly.

Sokolov blinked, momentarily thrown by the apparent non sequitur. "What?"

"A pizza," she said simply, her tone conversational despite the shiv still pressed against his throat. "Call this number and ask for an anchovy pizza."

Confusion spread across Sokolov's face, his brow furrowing as he tried to process this bizarre demand. "A... pizza? What are you talking about?"

Anna reached into her pocket with her free hand and withdrew a small, battered flip phone—the one she had taken from Nikolai's hidden cache beneath his mattress during the brief moments before the yard time. She placed it on the desk in front of Sokolov, screen facing up.

"This number," she said, nodding toward the phone. "Call it. Order the pizza. Anchovies. Specifically anchovies."

Sokolov stared at the phone as if it might explode. "This is absurd. We're in the middle of a maximum-security prison. There's a riot ongoing. And you want me to order a pizza?"

Anna increased pressure on the shiv, drawing another bead of blood. "I don't care if it makes sense to you. Do it."

Sokolov's eyes darted between her face and the phone, searching for understanding, for some hint of the strategy behind this seemingly random demand. Finding none, he slowly reached for the device, fingers trembling slightly.

"This is madness," he muttered, flipping the phone open.

Chapter 10

The Albino paced inside the isolated unit, frowning as he moved swiftly back and forth, speaking into his phone.

"So where is she now?" he demanded, his voice hoarse.

The response only made him angry.

"What do you mean you don't know?" He slammed his free hand against the wall, the impact barely registering. "Four men. She killed four of my best men in Odessa. Tortured Mikhail for twelve hours before he died." His colorless eyes narrowed to slits.

He resumed pacing, his movements becoming more agitated with each turn. The isolation cell—if it could even be called that—bore little resemblance to the concrete boxes that housed ordinary prisoners. Plush carpet covered the floor, absorbing the sound of his footsteps. A king-sized bed with Egyptian cotton sheets occupied one corner. A desk of polished mahogany stood against the far wall, its surface arranged with precision: laptop, satellite phone, leather-bound notebook. A climate control panel maintained the temperature at exactly 68 degrees—the Albino's preferred environment.

The cell door stood wide open. No bars, no reinforced steel—just an ordinary door that wouldn't look out of place in an upscale hotel. Beyond it, two guards stood at attention, their expressions carefully blank despite the one-sided conversation they couldn't help overhearing.

"You lost her trail in Belarus," the Albino continued, his voice dropping to a dangerous whisper. "Then Turkey. Then Kazakhstan. And now you tell me there's been no sign for three days?" He clicked his fingers sharply, the sound like a gunshot in the hushed space.

One of the guards immediately stepped forward, head bowed deferentially. "Sir?"

"Water," the Albino commanded without looking at him. "And tell the kitchen I want dinner at seven precisely. Not a minute before, not a minute after."

The guard nodded and withdrew, leaving his companion alone at the doorway. The Albino barely registered the exchange, his attention fixed on the voice coming through his phone.

"No, I don't care what resources it requires," he hissed, resuming his pacing. The thick carpet showed the wear patterns of his habitual movement—a figure eight that he traced and retraced as he thought, as he planned. "Find her. Use the FSB contacts if necessary. Call in the markers we have with GRU." He paused, listening, his pale face tightening. "No excuses. None."

He ended the call with a violent jab of his finger, tossing the phone onto the bed. For a moment, he stood perfectly still, only his eyes moving as they scanned the luxurious cell. Despite the amenities, despite the open door, despite the deferential guards, it was still a cage—a gilded, comfortable cage, but a cage...

He'd come here for protection, and... for a *meeting*. Calming himself, he rubbed at his temples and lowered his chin.

Tomorrow. The guest would arrive tomorrow.

A moment later, bereft of the previous signs of distress, he straightened himself, rolling his shoulders, his momentary frustration melting away as he contemplated tomorrow's meeting. His porcelain fingers traced the edge of his silk shirt—custom-made in Milan, the fabric so fine it felt like water against his skin. Everything in his life was custom. Tailored. Perfected. Nothing touched his body that hadn't been specifically designed for him, from the hand-stitched Italian leather shoes to the platinum cufflinks inlaid with rare blue diamonds.

He moved to the small bar in the corner of his cell—the word seemed absurd given the opulence surrounding him—and poured himself three fingers of Macallan 1926, a whisky so rare that a single bottle had sold at auction for $1.9 million. The crystal tumbler caught the light, refracting it across the walls in dancing patterns that seemed to entertain him momentarily.

"Everything has a price," he murmured to himself, swirling the amber liquid. "Everything and everyone."

The thought pleased him, smoothing the last edges of his irritation. This woman hunting him—this ghost who had eluded his best operatives—she too had a price. Everyone did. Some could be bought with money, others with power or protection or vengeance. But everyone had their breaking point, their price tag. It was simply a matter of discovering what currency they valued.

He sipped the whisky, savoring its complex notes, allowing himself a small smile. Tomorrow's meeting represented the culmination of decades of work, of careful manipulation, of strategic alliances and betrayals. The pieces were finally aligning—representatives from three governments, two cartels, and the shadow banking system that operated beyond the reach of international regulations. They had all played their part. But the meeting tomorrow? The special guest? This mattered more than anything. All coming together in this unlikely location, this prison that wasn't really a prison for him, but rather a fortress, a neutral ground where interests could converge without the scrutiny of intelligence agencies or regulatory bodies.

The Albino glanced at his watch—a Richard Mille RM 56-02 Tourbillon Sapphire worth over $2 million, its transparent case revealing the intricate mechanism within. Time moved differently for him than for others. While ordinary men counted hours and days, he measured his existence in empires built, markets manipulated, rivals eliminated.

"Sir," the remaining guard spoke from the doorway, his voice carefully modulated to convey respect without presumption. "Your secure line is ringing."

The Albino nodded once, returning to the desk where a second phone—this one encased in military-grade encryption hardware—vibrated silently against the polished wood. He lifted it to his ear without speaking, listening intently to the voice on the other end.

"Excellent," he said after several moments, his colorless eyes gleaming with satisfaction. "The final confirmation we needed." He listened again, his expression unchanged save for a slight tightening around his mouth. "No, I want the full shipment. Thirty percent is unacceptable. They either deliver as—"

The Albino continued his call, pausing mid-sentence as a piercing scream echoed through the isolation wing. The sound was distinctive—not the common shouts of prisoner frustration or the predictable wails of new inmates adjusting to confinement. This was something primal, a sound of genuine agony that cut through the prison's ambient noise like a blade.

His colorless eyes narrowed as he glanced toward the doorway. "What is that?" he demanded, interrupting whoever was speaking on the other end of the secure line.

The guard at the door shifted uncomfortably, his professional demeanor momentarily cracking. "New prisoner, sir. Brought in yesterday. Started a fight with the transport team—put three of them in the infirmary."

Another scream ripped through the isolation wing, this one somehow worse than the first—a sustained howl that seemed to contain words beneath the pain, though they were unintelligible at this distance.

The Albino's expression darkened, his features taking on an almost translucent quality in the subdued lighting. "Quiet him down," he commanded, voice dropping to a dangerous whisper. "I have important matters to discuss. Important calls to make."

"Yes, sir." The guard nodded sharply, relief evident in his posture at having been given a clear directive. He spoke into his radio, voice low and urgent. "Cell 14 needs immediate attention. Noise control protocol."

The Albino returned to his call, turning his back to the door as if physically dismissing the disturbance. "Apologies for the interruption," he said smoothly, his cultured voice betraying no hint of the irritation that had momentarily crossed his features. "As I was saying, the arrangement must be finalized before tomorrow's meeting. The documents require—"

A third scream interrupted him, this one different—less pain, more rage. Something crashed against a wall, the impact reverberating through the isolation wing's structure. The sound of running boots echoed in the corridor outside, guards responding to their colleague's summons.

The Albino's hand tightened around the phone, his knuckles standing out like white marble against already ghostly skin. "I'll call you back," he said tersely, ending the conversation without waiting for a response.

He moved to the doorway, stepping just past the threshold to observe the commotion down the corridor. Four guards hurried toward one of the isolation cells, batons drawn, faces set in grim determination. The cell in question—number 14 according to the small digital display beside its reinforced door—showed signs of disturbance. The observation window was smeared with what appeared to be blood.

"Who is in that cell?" the Albino demanded of a passing guard, his voice cutting through the chaos like a scalpel.

The guard froze, immediately straightening to attention despite the urgency of the situation. "A man named Kovac, sir. Transferred in yesterday. Former Spetsnaz."

"Well quiet him down. Now. I need everything in order. Do it. *Right now.*"

He scowled, turning back on his heel and approaching his phone once more. It didn't matter where the assassin was. She couldn't reach him in here.

And once he was done with tomorrow's meeting, he'd become the richest man in the world.

His lips twisted into a small smile.

Chapter 11

Sokolov sat rigidly at his desk, hands bound with his own silk tie, mouth sealed with premium duct tape from his personal supply drawer. The irony wasn't lost on Anna as she methodically transformed herself in the reflection of his office window. Outside, the last vestiges of the riot were being contained, distant shouts and occasional bangs providing a chaotic soundtrack to her precise movements.

The pizza box—delivered twenty minutes after Sokolov's reluctant call—contained no Italian food. Instead, nestled in professional-grade packaging, lay the tools of Anna's trade: a sleek brunette wig with auburn highlights, theatrical-grade makeup kit, a form-fitting black dress that could pass for business attire, stockings, and sensible yet elegant heels. Beneath these lay the more lethal contents—a ceramic blade thin enough to pass metal detectors, two syringes filled with clear liquid, a garrote wire disguised as an elegant necklace, and documentation so flawless even Sokolov had blinked in disbelief when she showed him.

And because it had been delivered to the warden, it had gone through a private entrance, an entry point devoid of available guards and weakened by the illusion that it was cut off from the chaos of the prison by the very series of locks and bottlenecks that Anna had crossed to reach the warden's office originally.

This was something they'd accounted for as well.

"Casper always delivers," Anna murmured as she applied a base layer of foundation, her fingers working with practiced efficiency. The makeup transformed her—softening the sharp angles of her face, creating contours where there were none, building a mask of femininity.

If a *prisoner* escorted the warden to the isolation wing, it would raise eyebrows.

But a beautiful female guest at the arm of the warden?

This was far less likely to raise any hackles. And by his reputation, Anna was counting on the guards' reluctance to question or interrupt the warden when he was enjoying the company of the fairer sex.

Sokolov watched with undisguised shock as Anna erased the masculine prisoner before his eyes. The foundation concealed the fading bruises from her prison fights. Contouring redefined her cheekbones, making them appear softer, more feminine. Eyeshadow in subtle earth tones made her green eyes seem larger, less predatory. Mascara lengthened lashes that were already naturally long. A neutral lipstick completed the illusion of a professional woman rather than a deadly operative.

The wig came next, settled with expert precision over her shaved head. The synthetic hair fell in natural-looking waves past her shoulders, the color chosen to complement her skin tone while being forgettable enough not to draw attention. She secured it with adhesive strips already attached on the inside, testing its stability with a quick shake of her head.

"The human mind is fascinating," Anna said conversationally as she slipped the dress from its tissue paper wrapping. "People see what they expect to see. A male prisoner with a shaved head becomes invisible when transformed into a well-dressed woman. Gender is perhaps the most effective disguise of all."

Sokolov made a muffled sound behind his gag, eyes widening as Anna stripped off her prison uniform without hesitation or modesty. She removed her chest strap. The dress slid over her body like liquid shadow, clinging to curves that had been hidden beneath the baggy prison garments. The fabric was a specialized blend—flexible enough for sudden movement, with hidden reinforced panels that could stop a knife thrust.

She stepped into the stockings, rolling them up with methodical precision. The heels added three inches to her height, changing her posture, her gait, her entire silhouette. She studied her reflection critically, adjusting minute details—a strand of hair, the angle of the dress's neckline, the position of the necklace that concealed a weapon.

When she finally turned to face Sokolov, the transformation was complete. The thin, pretty male prisoner was gone, replaced by an elegant, professional woman who could walk through the administrative wing of any government facility without raising an eyebrow. The warden's eyes widened further, disbelief evident despite his predicament.

She moved to the desk, her walk completely altered—a confident, feminine stride that bore no resemblance to the economical movements of the prisoner. From the pizza box, she withdrew a sleek leather folio and a government-issue ID badge on a lanyard. The documentation was impeccable—heavy cardstock with appropriate watermarks, official seals, and holograms that caught the light as she tilted them.

"Now," Anna said, leaning down to meet Sokolov's eyes, "I'm going to remove the tape. If you shout, if you try to alert anyone, I'll drive this—" she flashed the ceramic blade briefly, "—through your carotid artery. Death would follow in approximately ninety seconds. Quite messy. Quite painful. Do we understand each other?"

Sokolov glared at her with undisguised hatred, but after a moment, he gave a small nod.

Anna peeled the tape away in one swift motion. Sokolov winced but remained silent, working his jaw to restore circulation.

"You won't get away with this," he said, voice hoarse. "Every guard knows me. They'll realize—"

"They'll realize nothing," Anna interrupted smoothly. "You're going to escort me to the isolation wing as if I'm a perfectly legitimate visitor. The isolation wing that is supposedly closed for repairs." She smiled thinly. "You're going to tell them the ministerial inspection has been moved up due to the riot. An emergency evaluation."

He stared at her, shocked.

"We knew about that too," she said grimly. She needed him to think she held all the cards. She untied his hands, keeping the blade pressed against his side where his jacket would conceal it. "Stand slowly."

Sokolov rose, straightening his uniform jacket automatically, military habits reasserting themselves despite the situation. "This is insanity," he muttered. "The guards will never—"

"The guards will see what they expect to see," Anna cut him off again, sliding the lanyard over her head. "A beautiful woman on the arm of their commanding officer. A surprise inspection. Nothing to question." The ID badge displayed her photograph—though with longer hair and makeup—and identified her as Elena Vasilieva, Special Ministerial Inspector. Finished, she pressed the ceramic blade against his kidney, concealed from view by their bodies' proximity. "Now smile, Warden. We have an inspection to conduct."

Sokolov's face contorted into what might generously be called a grimace. "You're dead," he whispered through barely moving lips. "Whether today or tomorrow or next week. You're already dead."

"We all are," Anna replied, her voice eerily calm. "Some of us just have more work to do before we rest."

She guided him toward the door, her movements smooth and unhurried. The transformation wasn't just physical—her entire demeanor had shifted. The deadly efficiency of the prison fighter had been replaced by the poised confidence of a government official. She held the leather folio like a shield, a symbol of authority as potent as any weapon.

"One last thing," she murmured as Sokolov reached for the door handle. "If you try to signal the guards, if you attempt any code phrase or warning gesture, I'll kill you first and then as many of them as necessary. I didn't come this far to fail now."

The cold certainty in her voice seemed to finally penetrate Sokolov's resistance. Whatever he saw in her eyes—the absolute commitment, the willingness to die for her objective—made him swallow hard.

"You really want him that badly?" he asked, a note of genuine curiosity breaking through his fear and anger.

Anna's green eyes were unflinching. "I've crossed oceans of blood to reach him. What's a few more bodies?" She nodded toward the door. "Now. Take me to the Albino."

The hallway outside the warden's office was quiet, the administrative staff having evacuated during the riot. Anna stayed close to Sokolov, the blade a constant presence against his side as they moved through the carpeted corridors toward the security doors that separated the administrative wing from the prison proper.

The first checkpoint appeared ahead—a reinforced glass booth with a bored-looking guard monitoring security feeds. He straightened as they approached, eyes widening slightly at the sight of the warden accompanied by an unfamiliar woman.

"Sir," he acknowledged, gaze lingering on Anna before returning to Sokolov. "I wasn't informed of any visitors."

"Emergency inspection," Sokolov replied, his voice admirably steady despite the pressure against his kidney. "The ministry sent Inspector Vasilieva in response to the incident in the yard."

The guard frowned, glancing at his computer terminal. "I don't have any record of—"

"Do you think the ministry calls ahead during emergency evaluations, Officer?" Anna interjected, her Russian crisp and authoritative. She held up her ID badge, keeping it at just the right distance to be visible but not easily scrutinized. "The incident report indicated security failures at multiple levels. I need to assess the isolation wing immediately."

The guard hesitated, clearly uncomfortable with the protocol breach, but unwilling to directly challenge the warden. His eyes flicked between Sokolov's tight expression and Anna's confident posture.

"The isolation wing is closed for repairs, ma'am," he said finally, reaching for his radio. "Let me just confirm with security control that—"

"That won't be necessary," Sokolov interrupted, a bead of sweat visible at his temple. Anna increased pressure with the blade, feeling it press against the fabric of his uniform. "This inspection is classified. Ministry directive 1173. No radio communication."

The guard's hand froze halfway to his radio. His eyes widened slightly at the mention of the directive—a high-level security protocol that Anna had gambled would exist in some form. The slight relaxation in his shoulders confirmed her bet had paid off.

"Yes, sir," he said, reaching instead for the control panel. "Biometric confirmation required."

Sokolov leaned forward, placing his eye against a retinal scanner while simultaneously pressing his thumb to a fingerprint reader. Both devices beeped in confirmation, green lights illuminating on the control panel.

"Voice verification," an automated system announced. "State your name and authorization code."

"Sokolov, Viktor Andreevich," the warden stated clearly. "Authorization Zulu-Echo-Nine-Seven-Alpha."

The security door emitted a heavy thunk as magnetic locks disengaged. "Identity confirmed. Access granted," the system announced.

"Thank you, Officer," Anna said, offering the guard a professional smile as she guided Sokolov through the opening door. "Your cooperation will be noted in my report."

The guard nodded, still looking uncertain but unwilling to question his superior further. The heavy door sealed behind them with a pneumatic hiss, cutting off the administrative wing's carpeted comfort. They now stood in a transitional space—a sterile corridor with concrete floors and reinforced walls that marked the boundary between the prison's public face and its true nature.

"Not bad," Anna murmured as they moved forward. "Though your performance could use work. You're sweating."

Sokolov's jaw tightened. "There are two more checkpoints," he said through clenched teeth. "Each with more guards, more questions. You won't make it past the next one."

"We'll see," Anna replied, scanning the corridor ahead with professional assessment. Security cameras covered every angle, their red recording lights blinking steadily. Motion sensors were visible at regular intervals along the ceiling. "How many guards at the next checkpoint?"

"Three," Sokolov answered after a moment's hesitation. "All armed."

Anna nodded, processing this information without visible concern. "And the Albino's exact location?"

Sokolov's pace faltered slightly. "You can't possibly think—"

"His location," Anna repeated, the blade pressing deeper.

"High-security isolation," Sokolov finally responded, his voice dropping to a whisper. "Cell 12. But it's not... it's not what you think."

"Meaning?" Anna prompted, keeping her expression neutral as they approached a bend in the corridor.

"It's not a cell. It's a suite." Sokolov's face twisted with something between fear and disgust. "Custom furnishings. Personal chef. Communication equipment that would make most embassies jealous."

This confirmed what Anna had already suspected. The Albino wasn't a prisoner—he was a protected asset. A valuable commodity being kept safe within these walls, using the prison as cover for whatever operation was culminating tomorrow.

The corridor opened into a larger space where the second checkpoint stood—a reinforced station with bulletproof glass and three guards as Sokolov had described. All wore tactical gear, sidearms visible in holsters. Their attention sharpened as Anna and Sokolov approached, hands moving instinctively toward their weapons.

"Sir," the ranking officer acknowledged, eyes flicking to Anna with open suspicion. "The isolation wing is closed for—"

"Emergency inspection," Sokolov cut him off, repeating the cover story with marginally more conviction. "Inspector Vasilieva from the ministry. Classification level Crimson."

The senior guard frowned. "We received no notification of—"

"That's rather the point of an emergency inspection, isn't it?" Anna interjected, her tone professionally impatient. She opened the leather folio, revealing official-looking documents with ministry letterhead and multiple stamps. "The incident in the yard triggered automatic protocols. I need to verify the integrity of the isolation wing immediately."

The guard studied the documents, then Anna herself, his trained eyes noting details that might escape civilian observation. She maintained eye contact, projecting calm authority while computing exactly how quickly she could neutralize all three guards if necessary. The ceramic blade pressed against Sokolov's side was a constant reminder to the warden of the consequences of betrayal.

"I'll need to call this in," the guard said finally, reaching for a secure phone on the desk.

"That won't be possible," Anna replied smoothly. "This inspection falls under Directive 1173. No external communications until the assessment is complete."

The guard's hand hesitated over the phone. "Sir?" he asked, looking to Sokolov for confirmation.

A bead of sweat trickled down the warden's temple, but he gave a short nod. "Proceed with the verification protocols. The inspector's clearance is legitimate."

The senior guard still looked uncertain, but military discipline prevailed. He returned to the security console, activating the biometric systems. "Full identity verification required for both parties," he announced.

This was the moment Anna had anticipated—and dreaded. The biometric systems would immediately flag her as an impostor. No amount of makeup or documentation could fool retinal scans or fingerprint readers.

"Warden first," the guard instructed, gesturing to the biometric panel.

Anna's mind raced through contingencies. The moment Sokolov completed his verification, they would expect her to follow suit. The instant her biometrics failed to match any authorized personnel, alarms would trigger. She needed a different approach—immediately.

The guards here were heavily armed.

She scanned them, examining each. The guards didn't look threatened by her. That was their first mistake. Her appearance—the elegant dress, the carefully styled hair, the leather folio clutched like a shield—registered as 'bureaucrat' in their minds: a harmless 'female' who was probably some ministry pencil-pusher sent to file reports after the riot. Their body language betrayed their assessment: slightly relaxed postures, the casual way they kept their hands near but not on their weapons, the dismissive glances they exchanged.

"Ma'am, I understand you believe you have clearance," the senior guard said, his tone shifting to something almost patronizing, "but we have strict protocols here. Biometric verification is non-negotiable, especially for the isolation wing."

Anna allowed a flicker of frustration to cross her features—not the cold calculus of a trained operative, but the petulant annoyance of a government official whose authority was being questioned.

"This is absurd," she said, her voice rising slightly, taking on a nasal quality she hadn't used before. "I've been sent directly from Moscow. Do you understand the paperwork involved? The signatures? The minister himself signed these orders after the riot report reached his desk."

The youngest guard—barely twenty-five, with a fresh-faced eagerness that suggested recent academy graduation—shifted uncomfortably. "The system requires—"

"The system," Anna interrupted, stepping slightly away from Sokolov to gesture dramatically with her free hand, "is precisely what I'm here to evaluate! The riot occurred because of systemic failures, security breaches—protocol violations." She turned to the warden, maintaining the blade's pressure against his side while appearing to appeal to his authority. "Warden Sokolov, please explain to your men that ministerial authority supersedes local protocols during emergency evaluations."

The guards glanced toward Sokolov, seeking confirmation. The warden's face blanched, a sheen of sweat visible on his forehead, but he gave a short nod. "The inspector's clearance is valid," he managed, voice tight.

The senior guard still looked skeptical. "With respect, sir, we still need biometric confirmation from both of you. Those are standing orders from Central Command."

Anna sighed dramatically, the sound of an exasperated bureaucrat rather than a deadly operative. "Fine. The warden will proceed with his verification. But I must inform you that the riot has likely affected the security systems. My credentials were already verified at the main entrance and at the first checkpoint."

She glanced at her watch—an elegant timepiece that complemented her professional appearance. "Every minute we delay here is noted in my report. The minister is expecting preliminary findings by eighteen hundred hours."

The guards exchanged glances, their assessment of her solidifying: annoying ministry official, more concerned with reports and paperwork than real security. The most dangerous people often hide behind the most mundane facades, but this fundamental truth eluded them as they processed her apparent frustration.

"Proceed with your secondary verification, Warden," the senior guard instructed, gesturing to the biometric panel.

Sokolov stepped forward, Anna moving smoothly with him to maintain pressure with the concealed blade. As he leaned toward the retinal scanner, Anna took the opportunity to catalog their situation with clinical precision.

Three guards. The senior officer—mid-forties, former military judging by his bearing, right-handed, Makarov PM-12 sidearm in a quick-draw holster, combat knife visible at his ankle, radio clipped to his tactical vest. The youngest—nervous energy, weight shifted to his left leg suggesting possible right knee weakness, standard-issue MP-443 Grach pistol, finger already hovering near the trigger guard despite no immediate threat.

GUARDIAN'S MISSION

The third guard—heavyset, calm eyes that suggested experience, shotgun secured across his back, baton at his hip, positioning himself with clear sight lines to both entrances.

Beyond them, the security station contained two computer terminals, a weapons locker secured with a digital keypad, and emergency protocols posted on the wall—including evacuation routes. Three cameras covered the area, their positions creating a single blind spot near the left corner of the desk. The door leading further into the isolation wing required dual authentication—both a guard's verification and the warden's.

Anna calculated distances, angles, response times. If violence erupted, she would need to neutralize the senior guard first—his experience made him the greatest threat. The youngest would likely freeze momentarily, providing a critical second or two. The heavyset guard would be slower but potentially more dangerous in close quarters due to his size advantage.

"Identity confirmed," the automated system announced as Sokolov completed his biometric verification. "Secondary authentication required."

The senior guard nodded toward Anna. "Your turn, Inspector."

Anna smiled professionally, still projecting bureaucratic impatience rather than deadly focus. She glanced at the biometric panel, then at her watch again, building the performance of an official more concerned with time constraints than security procedures.

"As I explained," she began, reaching into her folio, "my credentials have already been—"

"Ma'am. Now, please."

She sighed.

No avoiding this confrontation. Cameras were pointed at her from six angles. She could feel them watching her. Once she acted, the riot control teams would be released. Local police would be called.

She'd be on a timer.

Another, longer sigh. Sometimes, a girl simply couldn't catch a break.

And then she moved with lethal efficiency.

Chapter 12

Anna's transformation from bureaucrat to assassin happened in the space between heartbeats.

Her first movement was almost gentle—she placed the leather folio on the security desk, as if finally acquiescing to the verification procedure. The senior guard relaxed fractionally, his hand moving away from his holster as he reached to activate the biometric scanner.

That microscopic relaxation was all she needed.

Anna's hand shot out with serpentine speed, fingers closing around the guard's wrist. Before he could register the attack, she twisted sharply, using his own momentum to slam his arm against the edge of the desk. Bone cracked with a sound like a dry branch snapping. As he gasped in shock, her other hand was already moving, fingers driving into his throat with surgical precision—collapsing his windpipe and temporarily sending him to his knees in a desperate fight for air.

The youngest guard's hand jerked toward his holster, eyes widening in stunned recognition that the elegant woman before him was something else entirely. Anna was already moving, her body a blur of blade-precise violence. She pivoted, leg sweeping upward in a kick that connected with his wrist just as his fingers closed around the grip of his pistol. The gun clattered across the floor as she completed the movement, driving her elbow into his solar plexus with enough force to expel all air from his lungs.

As he doubled over, she grabbed his head and brought it down to meet her rising knee. The impact was precisely calibrated to render him unconscious. He crumpled to the floor like a puppet with cut strings, blood streaming from his shattered nose.

Two down in less than three seconds.

The third guard—the heavyset one—had better reflexes than his companions. His shotgun was already swinging forward, fingers working the pump action with practiced efficiency. Anna launched herself toward him, using the desk as a springboard. Her body twisted in mid-air, a corkscrew of lethal grace that brought her feet first into his chest. The impact drove him backward against the wall, the shotgun discharging harmlessly into the ceiling as his finger reflexively squeezed the trigger.

Before he could recover, Anna's hands found the pressure points on either side of his neck, applying precise force to the carotid arteries. His eyes rolled back as blood flow to his brain was temporarily interrupted, consciousness fleeing in seconds.

She caught the shotgun as he slumped to the floor, pivoting to face Sokolov—only to find the warden had used the distraction to retrieve the fallen guard's pistol. He was already aiming, his military training evident in his stable grip and proper stance despite the sweat beading on his forehead.

She fired a split second before he did.

The shotgun's roar filled the confined space, its thunderous echo rebounding off concrete walls. Sokolov's eyes widened in shock as the blast caught him in the shoulder, spinning him. The pistol in his hand discharged harmlessly into the floor as he staggered backward, crimson blooming across his immaculate uniform.

"You..." he gasped, free hand clutching at the wound, incredulity written across his features. "You actually..."

Anna didn't waste breath responding. She was already moving, securing the fallen pistol and checking the guards. All three remained unconscious—alive, but thoroughly incapacitated. The shotgun blast would have triggered alarms throughout the prison system. Her timeline had just compressed dramatically.

She'd gone non-lethal... for now.

But she wasn't going to have that luxury on the way out. Riot teams would already be responding. Heavily armed guards in body armor with bullet proof shields would be coming—many of them.

She had to move.

"The isolation wing," she demanded, pressing the pistol against Sokolov's undamaged shoulder. "Open it. Now."

Blood seeped between the warden's fingers as he struggled to remain upright. His military bearing reasserted itself through the pain, spine straightening as he glared at her with naked hatred.

"You're dead," he whispered, voice tight with agony. "This facility will lock down automatically. Every guard, every—"

"I don't need every exit," Anna cut him off, her voice eerily calm despite the escalating situation. "I only need one path. To him."

"Final verification required," the automated system announced, its mechanical voice incongruously calm amid the chaos. "Secondary authentication needed."

Sokolov hesitated, assessment visible behind the pain in his eyes. Anna pressed the pistol harder against his wound, eliciting a hiss of agony.

"Your choice is simple," she said quietly. "Open the door or die here. Either way, I'm proceeding."

The warden's face contorted, a complex mixture of rage, fear, and resignation washing across his features. Finally, he nodded once—a sharp, military acknowledgment of reality. He moved to the control panel, leaving smears of blood on the pristine surface as he pressed his palm against the scanner.

"Sokolov, Viktor Andreevich," he stated, voice remarkably steady despite his injury. "Emergency override Crimson-Seven-Nine-Zero."

The heavy security door emitted a series of metallic clicks as multiple locks disengaged. "Override accepted," the system confirmed. "Warning: isolation wing security protocols suspended."

The door slid open silently, revealing a corridor beyond—sterile white walls, recessed lighting, and a distinct absence of the grime that characterized the rest of the prison. This was no ordinary isolation wing. It more closely resembled a high-security research facility or government bunker.

Anna's gaze swept the corridor, cataloging details with professional efficiency. Security cameras at regular intervals. Motion sensors embedded in the ceiling panels. Reinforced doors spaced evenly along both walls, each bearing a digital display indicating the cell number and occupant status.

"Move," she ordered, guiding Sokolov forward with the pistol. The warden stumbled slightly, his wounded shoulder leaving a trail of blood droplets on the immaculate floor. Emergency sirens had begun wailing in distant parts of the prison, the sound muffled by the isolation wing's substantial construction.

"You have perhaps two minutes," Sokolov said through gritted teeth as they moved deeper into the corridor. "The response team trains for situations like this. Former operators. They'll shoot to kill."

Anna didn't respond, her focus narrowing to the mission parameters. The digital displays on each door glowed with occupant information—most cells appeared empty, their status indicators showing green. Two displayed red, signifying occupied cells.

Cell 12. That was her target. The Albino's "suite," according to Sokolov.

Cell 14 showed red as well. Kovac. The man who had tried to kill her twice last week was here too. The coincidence felt wrong, like a dissonant note in an otherwise harmonious composition.

They reached a junction where the corridor branched in three directions. Sokolov swayed slightly, his face anemic from blood loss. "Left," he muttered, nodding toward the leftmost passage. "High-security section."

Anna hesitated, studying the warden's face for deception. Finding none, she nudged him forward along the indicated path. The new corridor was different—wider, better lit, with more sophisticated security measures visible at regular intervals. The floor transitioned from institutional tile to what appeared to be polished marble.

The incongruity was jarring—a luxury hotel hallway transplanted into the heart of a maximum-security prison. Recessed lighting cast a warm glow rather than the harsh fluorescents of the main corridor. The air carried a faint scent of sandalwood and expensive cologne rather than the antiseptic sterility of the outer wing.

At the end of this passage stood a final door—heavier than the others, its surface a burnished metal that reflected the light in rippling patterns. The digital display beside it read simply: "12 - OCCUPIED."

"This is it?" Anna asked, voice barely above a whisper.

Sokolov nodded once, his military bearing beginning to falter as shock set in. Blood had soaked the entire left side of his uniform now, dripping steadily onto the pristine floor.

"Guards?" she pressed, scanning the corridor for any sign of movement.

"Two," Sokolov answered, his voice growing weaker. "Inside. Always inside. Personal security, not prison staff." He laughed, a harsh sound that ended in a pained cough. "They don't work for me. They work for him."

Anna processed this information, recalculating her approach. Two unknown guards, likely highly trained if they served as the Albino's personal security. Unknown weapons, unknown capabilities. The element of surprise would be critical.

"Open it," she commanded, positioning Sokolov in front of her.

The warden swayed slightly, steadying himself against the wall with his good hand. "It requires... voice recognition. Biometric scan. And..." He hesitated.

"And?" Anna prompted, pressing the pistol against his spine.

"And his permission," Sokolov finished, nodding toward an intercom system beside the door. "He decides who enters. Always."

Anna's mind raced through options, discarding each as quickly as they formed. Using Sokolov as a human shield was the obvious approach, but if the Albino's guards were as professional as she suspected, they would be trained to prioritize their principal's safety over the warden's life.

The distant sirens grew louder. Time was running out.

An idea formed—dangerous, unorthodox, but potentially effective. She leaned close to Sokolov's ear, her voice a deadly whisper.

"Call him. Tell him you have Kovac. Tell him the prisoner from Cell 14 tried to escape, killed three guards, and that you've subdued him. Say you're bringing him for questioning because Kovac was asking about the Albino specifically."

Sokolov's eyes widened slightly—whether at the audacity of her plan or some other realization, she couldn't tell. "He won't believe—"

"He will if you make him believe," Anna cut him off. "Your life depends on it."

After a moment's hesitation, Sokolov nodded. He straightened as much as his injury allowed, composing his features into a semblance of official authority despite the pain evident in the tightness around his eyes. He pressed the call button on the intercom.

"Sir, this is Warden Sokolov," he began, his voice remarkably steady. "We've had an incident. The prisoner from Cell 14—Kovac—attempted escape. Three guards down. We've contained him, but..." He paused, glancing at Anna. "He was asking for you specifically. Claimed to have information about tomorrow's meeting."

The intercom remained silent for several agonizing seconds. Anna tensed, examining angles, escape routes, contingencies. The sirens continued their distant wail, growing incrementally louder as response teams navigated the prison's complex security systems.

Finally, a voice emerged from the speaker—cultured, precise, with the faint accent of someone who has learned multiple languages so perfectly that their original tongue has been diluted. "Kovac?" the voice murmured, a note of genuine curiosity evident despite the electronic distortion. "How... unexpected."

Anna felt a chill race along her spine at the sound. After months of hunting, of following trails of blood and corruption across continents, she was finally hearing the Albino's voice directly. Not a recording, not a secondhand account, but the man himself.

"Yes, sir," Sokolov continued, sweat beading on his forehead from both pain and fear. "He became violent during transport. Kept repeating your name. Said he had information about the Turkish operation that you would want to hear personally."

Another pause, longer this time. Anna could almost feel the considerations happening on the other side of that door, the weighing of risks and opportunities, the cold assessment of potential threats against potential gains.

"Bring him in," the voice finally replied. "But Warden, ensure he is properly restrained. I remember Kovac from Ankara. He is... unpredictable."

A series of mechanical clicks emanated from the heavy door as multiple locks disengaged. Anna positioned herself behind Sokolov, the pistol pressed against his spine but concealed from anyone who might be watching through security cameras or the door's viewing panel.

"Move," she whispered, her lips barely moving. "Slowly. Keep talking as we enter."

The door swung inward with the silent precision of expensive engineering. The contrast between the prison corridor and what lay beyond was jarring—like stepping from a military facility into a luxury penthouse. Plush carpet covered the floor, absorbing the sound of their footsteps. The walls were paneled in rich wood rather than institutional concrete. Recessed lighting cast a warm glow over furniture that wouldn't have looked out of place in a five-star hotel suite.

And there, standing in the center of this incongruous luxury, was the Albino.

He was taller than Anna remembered, his slender frame giving the impression of a dancer rather than a criminal mastermind. His skin was indeed unnaturally pale, almost translucent in places, revealing the tracery of blue veins beneath. White hair, cut with precision, framed features that might have been handsome if not for the complete absence of warmth in his colorless e yes.

Those eyes fixed on Anna immediately, widening slightly as they registered not the expected prisoner but a woman in an elegant black dress, holding a pistol against the warden's back. Recognition flashed across his face—not of Anna specifically, but of the situation—the trap.

Two guards flanked him, their reactions professionally swift. Hands moved toward concealed weapons, bodies shifting to protective stances. But they hesitated, caught between training that demanded immediate neutralization of the threat and uncertainty about risking their principal's safety with crossfire.

That momentary hesitation was all Anna needed. Her arm extended in one fluid motion, the pistol clearing Sokolov's shoulder as she fired. The report was deafening in the confined space, the sound incongruously violent amid the luxury surroundings. Her first shot caught the guard to the Albino's right—a precise impact that found the narrow gap between tactical vest and collar, punching through his throat. Arterial blood sprayed in a crimson arc across the pristine carpet as he dropped, hands clutching futilely at his ruined neck.

The second guard was faster, his training evident in the economy of his movements. As his companion fell, he was already firing, his weapon materializing in his hand as if conjured from thin air. His first shot went wide, embedding itself in the wooden paneling beside the door. His second found Sokolov's chest, the impact lifting the warden off his feet and throwing him backward. The bullet punched through his sternum, shredding his heart before exiting through his spine in a spray of bone fragments and tissue.

Sokolov was dead before he hit the floor, his body collapsing in a boneless heap that spilled fresh blood across the expensive carpet. His eyes remained open, fixed in an expression of stunned disbelief that would never change.

Anna was already moving, dropping into a crouch as she sought a clean shot at the remaining guard. The Albino, however, displayed a physical prowess that belied his ethereal appearance. With surprising strength, he grabbed his surviving bodyguard by the tactical vest and shoved him bodily toward Anna, using him as both shield and weapon.

The guard—a heavyset man whose muscular frame suggested years of physical training—careened into Anna with the force of a battering ram. The impact knocked her backward, sending both her pistol and her breath ejecting from her as they crashed to the floor in a tangle of limbs. The back of her head connected with the marble entryway, stars exploding across her vision as the guard's substantial weight drove the air from her lungs.

Instinct took over where conscious thought faltered. Anna's hand found the ceramic blade concealed at her thigh, drawing it in a movement so practiced it required no visual guidance. The guard was recovering quickly, his training evident in how swiftly he regained his bearings. His hand closed around her throat, fingers seeking the pressure points that would render her unconscious in seconds.

The blade slipped between his ribs, angled upward to find the heart. His eyes widened, mouth opening in a silent gasp as the ceramic edge severed cardiac tissue. Anna twisted the blade once, ensuring catastrophic damage before withdrawing it in a single smooth motion. Blood welled from the wound, soaking through his tactical vest as his grip on her throat loosened.

She shoved the dying man aside, rolling swiftly to her feet despite the throbbing pain in her skull. Her hands came up, leveling the pistol toward the line she'd seen the Albino darting along—the pistol barrel sweeping across the wall of the suite until it reached the rapidly closing crack of a metal door.

Two pink eyes glared at her. She fired and the door shut. The bullet sparked off the metal. And then, the suite went still once more.

"Shit," she whispered under her breath.

The alarms blared deeper in the prison.

Two minutes. That's what she'd been told. There was a two minute response time, and then this hall would be flooded with heavily armed men in riot gear.

Chapter 13

Anna stared at the door. She had been so *close.* She *was* so close. The Albino was hidden just behind it—biometrics and magnetic locks reading with red lock-out icons in the frame—while riot teams were now swiftly moving towards her position.

Taking a breath, Anna assessed, returning to the suite's hall entrance and glancing up and down the corridor beyond.

She couldn't waste time on frustration. The mission parameters had changed; adaptation was essential. The Albino was temporarily beyond reach behind that reinforced door, and armored teams were closing in to rescue him. She needed a new approach.

Blood pooled around her feet from the two dead guards and Warden Sokolov's corpse, making the pristine marble entrance to the Albino's suite resemble an abattoir. Anna quickly searched the bodies, retrieving the other guard's sidearm—a custom Glock with a suppressor already attached. Professional equipment for professional killers.

The time for bluffs had passed, and stripping her heels, Anna gave her dress a quick tear to free up the movement of her legs. Dragging a pair of boots from the leanest of the dead men around her, she propped herself against the door and glanced outside as she cinched the more resilient footwear with military precision.

Her gaze swept the corridor, weighing options. The isolation wing's design meant limited exit routes—all likely being filled with armed response teams at this moment. The sirens had changed tone, shifting to a higher pitch that indicated a full facility lockdown. Standard procedure would involve sealing all sectors, flooding corridors with armed personnel, establishing a perimeter, then methodically clearing each area.

She needed leverage: information, a bargaining chip.

Maybe she could negotiate with the Albino?

Hell no.

The thought was rejected almost as soon as it was formed. She wasn't even willing to try talking to him.

So?

She sighed, glancing down to the only other occupied cell. She let out a slow breath.

He'd tried to kill her. Had tried to kill her sister, to kill Casper... He had led a breaching team onto a private yacht, murdering the captain of the ship.

"Dammit," she whispered under her breath.

She was almost out of options. What else was there? What could she leverage if not—?

Cell 14. Kovac.

The coincidence of his presence nagged at her tactical assessment. Had he tried to follow her here? Was he still after her?

Soon. That's what he'd muttered. He was focused, the same way she was. How could she negotiate with someone as bullheaded as herself?

It didn't matter. She was out of options. That same determination left her with *no* choice.

Decision made, Anna moved swiftly back down the marble hallway toward the junction where the corridor split. Blood had soaked through her stockings, the sensation unpleasantly familiar against her skin. The dress—designed for infiltration rather than combat—now sported tears along the seams where she'd fought the guard.

At least she'd thrown away the wig.

Reaching the junction, she paused, listening. Distant shouts echoed through the isolation wing—response teams coordinating their approach. Based on the acoustics, they hadn't yet breached the inner security doors. Perhaps thirty seconds before visual contact.

She turned right, moving toward Cell 14 with purposeful strides. The digital display glowed red: "OCCUPIED - MAXIMUM SECURITY PROTOCOL."

Unlike the Albino's luxurious suite, this was a traditional isolation cell—a reinforced door with a small observation window, electronic lock requiring key card access. Through the window, Anna could see a man seated on a metal bench bolted to the wall. His head was bowed, hands clasped between his knees. Blood matted his dark hair, staining the collar of his prison uniform. Evidence of recent beating was visible in the swelling across his f ace.

Anna assessed the lock system—standard prison-grade electronic mechanism with key card reader and emergency override keypad. She turned, breaking into a sprint back towards Sokolov's body.

She needed his keycard, and she needed it fast.

The alarm sirens wailed as Anna raced back to Sokolov's cooling body. She rolled him onto his side, fingers swiftly searching his pockets. Her hands came away bloody, but she found what she needed—a master access card clipped to his belt beneath his jacket.

Footsteps and shouted commands echoed down the corridor—closer now. The response team had breached the outer security doors. She had perhaps twenty seconds before they reached the junction.

Anna sprinted back to Cell 14, swiping the keycard through the reader. The light flashed green, and the lock disengaged with a heavy thunk. She pushed the door open, weapon raised and stepped inside.

Kovac didn't look up immediately. His posture remained unchanged—head bowed, hands clasped between his knees, a picture of defeated resignation. Only when the door clicked shut behind her did he raise his head.

His face was a map of recent violence. One eye was swollen completely shut, the tissue around it purple and distended. A split lip had crusted with dried blood. Fresh bruises bloomed across his cheekbones and jaw. But his open eye—icy, almost colorless—fixed on her with immediate recognition.

"You," he said, his voice a rasping whisper through damaged vocal cords. "The ghost."

Anna kept the weapon trained on him, maintaining distance. "On your feet. Now."

Kovac smiled, the expression grotesque through his battered features. "Always so direct." He rose slowly, his movements revealing additional injuries—broken ribs perhaps, judging by how he favored his left side.

"Hands where I can see them," Anna commanded.

He complied, raising bloodstained hands to shoulder height. His prison uniform hung loosely on his frame, torn in places, revealing glimpses of bandages and additional bruising beneath. Whatever interrogation he'd endured had been thorough.

"You're bleeding," he observed, nodding toward her legs where the guard's blood had soaked through her stockings. "Not yours, I think."

"We don't have time for pleasantries." She flung one of the guns at Kovac.

He caught it on instinct. Stared at it, then looked slowly up, like a shark having just spotted a minnow. He even slowly licked his lips.

"That gun," she said quickly, realizing she had less than twenty seconds to make a pitch that spared her life and completed the mission, "was used to kill a guard. Now your fingerprints are on it. I can't shoot my way out of this alone. I need covering fire. Someone good at what they do."

He just stared at her, tense.

"It's loaded," she said simply. "I'm not lying. If you shoot me now, you'll accomplish your mission. But they'll kill you. If you help me, you'll survive too. And then you can have your chance at me later."

She wasn't sure the self-preservation pitch would matter. Kovac didn't seem the sort who cared much about living or dying.

Ten seconds. Voices now shouting. They were nearing the junction. She aimed over her shoulder and fired multiple shots.

Buying a few precious seconds.

Kovac's smile widened, splitting his lip anew. Blood trickled down his chin as he weighed the weapon in his hand, testing its balance with the casual familiarity of someone who had held many such tools throughout his life.

"You've changed your appearance," he noted, his voice eerily calm despite the chaos unfolding around them. "The dress suits you better than prison clothes. Though the blood is a familiar touch."

The shouting in the corridor grew louder. Heavy boots pounded against concrete, tactical teams coordinating their approach with professional efficiency. Anna fired another suppressed shot down the hallway, not aiming to hit anyone, but to slow their advance.

"Decision time," she said, her own voice matching his calm. "Help me escape, and you can try to kill me later. Fight me now, and we both die here."

Kovac's undamaged eye studied her face, searching for deception, calculation evident in his gaze. "You had your chance to kill me on the yacht," he said finally. "You chose not to. Why?"

"That wasn't the mission," Anna replied simply.

"And now?"

"Now I need to reach the Albino. He's in Cell 12. Behind a reinforced door with biometric locks."

Something flickered across Kovac's battered face—recognition, perhaps, or confirmation of a suspicion. "The Albino," he repeated, the name carrying weight beyond its syllables. "Of course. It makes sense now."

"Your answer?" Anna pressed, checking the magazine in her own weapon. "They'll be here in seconds."

Kovac straightened, seeming to shed some of his apparent weakness like a snake shedding skin. His posture shifted, muscles tensing beneath the prison uniform. The transformation was subtle but unmistakable—a monster awakening.

"I accept your terms," he said, chambering a round with practiced efficiency. "Temporary alliance. We both want out of this prison alive."

Anna didn't waste time questioning his motives or the sincerity of his agreement. The tactical reality demanded immediate action, not psychological analysis. She moved to the door, peering through the observation window to assess the corridor.

They were here.

"Response team at the junction," she reported, counting silhouettes. "Six men, tactical gear, assault rifles. Standard breach formation."

Kovac joined her at the door, his movements more fluid now, as if the prospect of violence had somehow alleviated the pain of his injuries. "Approach strategy?" he asked, the question revealing his own tactical training.

"We need a diversion," Anna replied, her mind racing through options. "Something to split their attention."

Her gaze fell on the control panel beside the door—not just for Cell 14, but a master panel that monitored all cells in this section of the isolation wing. An emergency override button was protected by a thin plastic cover.

"Prison riot protocol," she murmured, a plan forming. "What happens if all cells in isolation suddenly unlock?"

"Only two cells in isolation are occupied," he warned her.

"Maximum, yes. Here, yes. But other isolation units—lower priority ones. I passed them on the way in."

Kovac's undamaged eye glinted with understanding. "Chaos," he replied, a note of appreciation in his voice. "They'll have to divide forces between containing potential escapees and pursuing us."

Anna nodded. "Cover me."

She moved swiftly to the control panel, examining it with practiced efficiency. The emergency override required a key—likely one Sokolov would have carried. There was no time to retrieve it. Instead, she pried open the plastic cover and examined the wiring beneath.

"Thirty seconds," Kovac warned, positioning himself by the door. "They're advancing methodically. Room-by-room search."

Anna's fingers worked with surgical precision, identifying the circuits that controlled the locking mechanisms. Standard prison architecture included fail-safes—systems designed to prevent mass releases during power failures or emergencies. But every system had vulnerabilities if you knew where to look.

"This model has a bypass relay," she muttered, more to herself than Kovac. "Cross the primary circuit with the emergency power..."

Her hands moved swiftly, stripping wires, creating connections that the designers never intended. Sparks flashed as she completed the circuit, causing the panel to emit a series of warning beeps.

"System override initiated," an automated voice announced. "Emergency protocol engaged."

Throughout the isolation wing, locks disengaged with simultaneous metallic clicks. Doors remained closed but unlocked, awaiting only a push to open.

"Now we wait," Anna said, moving back to the door.

They didn't have to wait long. Confused shouts echoed down the corridor as the response team realized what was happening. Orders were barked, formations broken as guards rushed to secure what they believed were multiple prison breaks in progress.

"Five seconds," Kovac counted down, his voice taking on an almost eager quality. "Four... three..."

They both stared from their position behind the guard desk, down the hall. They could just make out prison doors at the end of the hall.

The first prisoner emerged from his cell—a heavyset man with prison tattoos visible on his neck and hands. He looked confused, hesitant, uncertain if his suddenly unlocked door represented freedom or a trap. When no immediate response came from the guards, who were now divided between multiple potential threats, he made his decision. He ran.

Others followed his example. Three more prisoners emerged from cells further down the corridor, each making their own choice about which direction offered the best chance of escape. Shouts intensified as guards attempted to respond to multiple threats simultaneously.

Anna remained crouched behind the cover of the guard position. The security panel sparked above her. Kovac breathed heavily at her side, as if inhaling her scent. He clutched the gun in his hand, then checked the round in the chamber with expert precision.

Across from them, the door to cell 14 remained open.

The first group from the responding riot team appeared by the open door, peering in, weapons held over their shields.

A brief opportunity. Their backs turned.

No way out but through.

"We need their grenades and shields," she whispered.

"Understood."

Three more members of the riot team now caught up. Other voices shouted from where prisoners were escaping.

More riot teams were delayed. But not for long.

She had no room for non-lethal techniques this time. Blood was the only way through.

"Now," Anna whispered, and they moved as one.

Kovac emerged from their hiding place first, his movements showing that ghoulish fluidity that seemed to ignore the pain of his injuries. He fired twice—precise shots that found the gaps in the first guard's body armor, hitting the vulnerable area where arm met torso. The man dropped with a strangled cry, his rifle clattering across the floor.

Anna followed, staying low, using Kovac's larger frame as partial cover. She targeted the second guard, her suppressed shot catching him in the thigh where the tactical armor didn't extend. He stumbled, shield wavering, creating an opening that Anna exploited immediately. Her second shot found his throat, ending his struggle.

The remaining guards reacted with professional speed, shields interlocking to form a barrier as they backed toward the junction. One reached for a radio, mouth opening to call for reinforcements.

Kovac moved with lethal grace, vaulting over a fallen guard and using the momentum to drive his shoulder into the shield wall. The unexpected impact broke their formation, sending one guard staggering backward. Kovac's gun pressed against the man's chin, firing upward through the soft tissue into his brain.

Anna rolled beneath a shield as its bearer struggled to maintain position, coming up inside the guard's defense. Her ceramic blade flashed, finding the femoral artery with surgical precision. Blood fountained as she twisted away, already targeting her next opponent.

The corridor became a swirl of controlled violence, bullets ricocheting off walls, shields clattering against the floor. Anna and Kovac moved with uncanny coordination, as if they'd trained together for years rather than being mortal enemies until minutes before. Each anticipated the other's movements, creating openings, exploiting vulnerabilities, their deadly dance leaving broken bodies in its wake.

A guard managed to throw a flashbang grenade, the device skittering across the floor toward them. Kovac kicked it without breaking stride, sending it back toward its source. The detonation filled the corridor with blinding light and deafening sound, but Anna and Kovac had already turned away, eyes closed, ears protected by forearms raised at precisely the right moment.

The disoriented guards were easy targets. Anna claimed a shield from a fallen officer, using it to advance toward the junction while Kovac provided covering fire. His marksmanship was impressive—each shot finding vulnerable points despite his swollen eye and the chaotic conditions.

They reached the junction, breathing hard but moving with purpose. The isolation wing had descended into complete chaos. Prisoners from the lower-security cells had engaged with guards, creating multiple skirmishes throughout the area. Alarms continued their piercing wail, emergency lights casting everything in pulsing red illumination.

"Which way?" Kovac asked, reloading with ammunition taken from a fallen guard.

Anna oriented herself, mentally mapping the facility based on her entry route. "Back."

"Back?"

"The Albino."

He smirked at her. "A hound with a scent?"

"You understand."

A nod.

"Grab grenades. Riot shields. Helmets. Automatic weapons."

Kovac was already nodding, moving to comply with the directive as Anna followed her own instruction.

A guard further down the hall looked up, spotting her. He shouted, taking aim, but she shot him first. A bullet to the throat. As the guard dropped, his warning died, drowned while blood filled his lungs. Anna moved quickly to retrieve his equipment, stripping him of his tactical vest and radio.

"Riot team three, report," a voice crackled through the radio. "What's your status? Respond immediately."

Anna ignored it, slinging an assault rifle across her back and securing additional magazines to the vest. Kovac appeared beside her, similarly equipped now, his battered face partially concealed by a tactical helmet.

"Ready?" she asked, checking her weapons one final time.

Kovac nodded, something like anticipation gleaming in his undamaged eye. "To Cell 12, then."

They moved with synchronized efficiency back toward the marble corridor, stepping over bodies they had left in their wake. The luxury section housing the Albino's suite remained sealed, the heavy door closed and likely reinforced from within

"Biometric locks," she explained as they approached. "Sokolov's access won't work now. The Albino will have locked down completely."

"Then we make our own door," Kovac replied, patting a bandolier of grenades he'd collected from the fallen guards. "Shaped charges. Military grade."

Anna assessed the explosives, then the door. "It's reinforced. Probably blast-resistant."

"Everything breaks eventually," Kovac said, his voice taking on an almost philosophical quality. "It's just a matter of finding the right pressure point." He began arranging the grenades in a specific pattern against the door's hinges and locking mechanism, his hands moving with the practiced efficiency of someone who had demolished many such barriers.

The radio on Anna's vest crackled again, more urgent now. "All units, be advised. Isolation wing compromised. Multiple officers down. Two armed suspects, considered extremely dangerous. Shoot on sight authorization granted."

Anna kept watch as Kovac worked, her mind racing through their next steps. Even if they breached the Albino's door, they would still need to fight their way out of a prison in full lockdown. Escape routes would be sealed, external reinforcements already arriving.

"Wire set," Kovac announced, stepping back from his handiwork. "Ten-second delay after triggering."

Anna nodded, positioning herself against the wall adjacent to the door, shield raised. Kovac mirrored her stance on the opposite side, producing a small detonator from among his collected equipment.

"Three, two, one," he counted down, then pressed the trigger.

The explosion was controlled but substantial, the shaped charges directing their force precisely where needed. The door didn't disintegrate as much as it was surgically removed from its frame, hinges and locking mechanisms shearing away in a shower of superheated metal.

The inner room of the luxury suite was dark now, emergency lighting casting eerie shadows across opulent furnishings. Smoke from the explosion hung in the air, mingling with the scent of cordite and sandalwood cologne. Anna advanced cautiously, shield raised, scanning for threats.

The Albino was gone.

Where he had stood minutes earlier was now empty space. The suite appeared undisturbed save for the destruction at the entrance—the expensive carpet still pristine beyond the blast radius, furniture arranged with mathematical precision, not a single object out of place. It was like a magician's cabinet trick—close the door and he disappears.

"Impossible," Anna muttered, advancing further into the room. Her eyes darted to corners, doorways, potential hiding spots. "There's no other exit."

Kovac moved to her left, his movements predatory as he swept his sector. "There's always another exit," he said quietly. "Men like him ensure it."

They moved deeper into the suite's inner room, passing from the main living area into what appeared to be a bedroom. A king-sized bed with fine sheets of Egyptian cotton stood untouched, pillows still perfectly arranged. An antique desk occupied one corner, its surface bare except for a single leather-bound notebook.

Beyond, a marble bathroom gleamed in the emergency lighting, its fixtures gold-plated, shower large enough for four people. No sign of the Albino.

"Here," Kovac called from beside a bookcase filled with leather-bound volumes. His fingers traced the edge of the shelving unit, finding imperceptible seams. "Hidden door. Recently used."

Anna joined him, examining the mechanism. The craftsmanship was exceptional—no visible hinges, no obvious handle or lock. The door was designed to disappear completely into the surrounding décor.

"How do we open it?" she asked, fingers probing the edges.

Kovac studied the bookcase, his single functioning eye narrowed in concentration. On a shelf rested a glass display box holding an ancient-looking book in leather binding and tooled with the title *Il Principe*. He reached for the display case, twisting it aside to reveal a hidden switch. The conceit of the concealing book was not lost on Anna. It was a first edition of Machiavelli's *The Prince*.

As Kovac flipped the switch, something clicked within the wall. The bookcase shifted silently, revealing a narrow passage beyond.

"Old tradecraft," Kovac explained, a note of professional appreciation in his voice. "The classics endure for a reason."

Anna glanced at him sharply. "How did you know?"

His battered face twisted into what might have been a smile on a less damaged visage. "Because if men like him ever cease being condescendingly clever, they simply burst into flames."

The passage was narrow but well-lit by recessed LED strips that activated as the door opened. It sloped gently downward, the walls concrete rather than the wood paneling of the suite. Air flowed from below, cool and slightly damp.

"Maintenance tunnel?" Anna guessed, checking her weapon before entering.

Kovac nodded. "Probably connects to utilities access. Old prisons like this often have infrastructure dating back decades. Forgotten passages. Unofficial routes."

They entered the tunnel single file, Anna leading with her shield still raised, Kovac following closely. The two mortal enemies set off in pursuit of the arm's dealer.

Chapter 14

The Albino ran through the dark, sweating. He hated sweating. All around him, the dingy tunnel echoed with the sound of his expensive Italian leather shoes striking concrete, each impact sending jolts of discomfort up his spine. The emergency lighting cast his shadow in grotesque elongations against the curved walls—a specter fleeing through the bowels of the earth.

Sweat trickled down his neck, soaking into the collar of his custom silk shirt. The sensation revolted him. Perspiration was for lesser beings—for the guards, the prisoners, the expendable masses whose bodily functions remained uncontrolled and animalistic. His own body's betrayal felt like an insult, a reminder of the humanity he worked so diligently to transcend.

"Disgusting," he muttered, withdrawing a monogrammed handkerchief to dab at his forehead as he ran. Even in flight, certain standards had to be maintained.

Ancient pipes ran along the ceiling, dripping condensation at irregular intervals. The occasional rat skittered away from his approach, their primitive instincts recognizing a more dangerous scavenger.

His pale fingers fumbled with his satellite phone, the device slick in his sweating hands. This wasn't supposed to happen. Not today. Not when everything was so perfectly arranged. Years of planning, of manipulation, of careful positioning of assets and elimination of obstacles—all jeopardized because one woman had somehow penetrated his sanctuary.

The phone connected with a soft beep, encryption protocols engaging automatically.

"It's me," he hissed into the device, not bothering with identification. Anyone who had this number knew precisely who he was. "Emergency extraction. Now."

"Sir," a clipped voice responded, professional and emotionless. "Your scheduled departure is tomorrow after—"

"Does this sound like a scheduled situation?" the Albino snapped, his cultured voice cracking slightly. A rivulet of sweat traced the contour of his spine, further fueling his fury. "The prison has been compromised. She's here."

There was a pause on the other end—brief but noticeable. "Understood, sir. Extraction team is twenty minutes out. Proceed to the designated point and—"

"No," the Albino cut them off, taking a sharp left where the tunnel branched. He knew these passages intimately, having memorized the facility's blueprints long before arranging his 'incarceration' here. "The original extraction point is compromised. She'll anticipate it."

He paused at another junction, orienting himself. The maintenance tunnels formed a labyrinthine network beneath the prison—some dating back to the facility's construction in the Soviet era, others added during various renovations. Most had been forgotten by the current administration, existing only in classified architectural archives that the Albino had paid handsomely to acquire.

The Albino reached another junction, this one marked with faded Cyrillic lettering that identified an old maintenance access. His mind considered routes, alternatives, contingencies—the mental map of the facility expanding and contracting as he eliminated options. Twenty minutes was far too long. She would be following. He had seen enough of her handiwork across three continents to know she wouldn't stop. Once she was through the magnetic locks on the steel door to his bedroom, he was uncertain if the bookcase would even slow her down.

"Listen carefully," he said into the phone, his voice regaining its customary precision. "I'm rerouting to emergency extraction point Omega. The secondary tunnel system beneath the old boiler room. And I want everything. Understand? Everything."

"Sir, protocol dictates—"

"I don't care about protocol," the Albino hissed, his colorless eyes narrowing as he pictured the faceless operator on the other end of the line. Another expendable piece. "The woman who breached my security killed two of my personal guards in less than six seconds. She navigated a maximum-security prison during a lockdown."

He paused at another intersection, calculating. The air was different here—mustier, with undertones of diesel fuel and rust. Older sections of the tunnel network. Less used. Less likely to be on any current prison schematics.

"I want a full tactical team," he continued, his voice dropping to a dangerous whisper. "Armored vehicles. Air support on standby. And alert our assets in the interior ministry—I want local authorities diverted, not converging. Create an incident elsewhere if necessary."

The operator's voice changed subtly, a new note of understanding—or perhaps fear—entering their previously professional tone. "Understood, sir. Full package deployment to Omega. ETA eighteen minutes."

"And the meeting?" the Albino asked, his mind already adjusting plans, considering probabilities, adapting to this unwelcome disruption.

"Sir?"

"Tomorrow's meeting," he clarified, irritation sharpening his words. "Contact all parties. Location change. The secondary site in Murmansk."

"But sir, several delegates are already en route to—"

"Do I sound like I'm asking for opinions?" The Albino's voice remained quiet but acquired a brittle edge that silenced the operator immediately. "Murmansk. The facility is secure, isolated, and most importantly, not compromised. Anyone who can't adapt to changing circumstances isn't worth my time or investment."

"Yes, sir. I'll notify all parties immediately."

The Albino ended the call, sliding the phone back into his pocket. Eighteen minutes to extraction. The woman—Anna, if his intelligence was correct—would be in pursuit by now. Possibly with Kovac. It was an unexpected complication, those two finding each other. His arrival in isolation was fortuitous, far too much to be a coincidence. That would bear looking into—later, once he'd made good his escape.

The Albino quickened his pace, each footfall echoing in the confined space of the tunnel. The pristine soles of his Italian leather shoes—handcrafted by an octogenarian cobbler in Milan who made only twelve pairs annually—were already ruined, collecting grime and moisture from the neglected passageway. Another loss to add to the ledger, another debt this woman would pay.

He reached into his pocket, extracting a small silver case. Inside lay two pills—one white, one blue. Emergency measures for extraordinary circumstances. He swallowed the white one dry, grimacing at the bitter taste and the primitive act of ingesting a substance without water. The stimulant would sharpen his senses, accelerate his thought processes, and provide a temporary boost to his physical capabilities. The blue pill remained in the case—a final option he hoped not to require.

The tunnel widened slightly as he entered a section that paralleled the prison's ancient sewage system. The ceiling rose high enough that he could stand at his full height, no longer forced into the undignified half-crouch of the maintenance passages. Rusty pipes ran along the walls, occasionally releasing jets of steam from failing gaskets. The temperature had risen several degrees, causing fresh beads of perspiration to form on his alabaster skin.

And then he heard it. Footsteps. Not the measured tread of his extraction team arriving early, but the swift, purposeful stride of pursuit. Two sets—one heavier, one lighter. They were moving fast— extremely fast. The acoustics of the tunnel system distorted distance, but his trained ear estimated they were perhaps two hundred meters behind him and closing rapidly.

"Impossible," he whispered, his pink eyes widening slightly. He had chosen the most obscure route, one documented only in architectural plans secured in KGB archives decades ago. Yet somehow, they had tracked him.

The Albino abandoned any pretense of dignity then, breaking into a full sprint. The stimulant was taking effect, his heart rate increasing to pump oxygenated blood to his muscles more efficiently. His vision sharpened, the dim emergency lighting suddenly appearing adequate as his pupils dilated to their maximum capacity.

The footsteps behind him accelerated in response, an unmistakable message: I hear you. I'm coming for you.

He reached into his pocket, withdrawing the satellite phone again. "Fifteen minutes is unacceptable," he hissed the moment the connection established. "I need extraction now."

"Sir, the team is moving at maximum speed," the operator responded, their voice tight with stress. "Air assets are scrambling, but the prison's location makes approach difficult."

The Albino rounded a corner, nearly colliding with a rusted maintenance cart abandoned decades earlier. He vaulted over it with surprising agility for his slender frame, the stimulant granting him physical capabilities normally beyond his reach.

The tunnel abruptly opened into a larger chamber—an old pumping station, its massive machinery long since abandoned but still dominating the space like industrial sculptures. Massive pipes disappeared into the walls, ceiling, and floor, creating a three-dimensional maze of metal. The air was warmer here, heavy with moisture and the lingering ghosts of diesel fumes.

The Albino paused, calculating. The chamber offered multiple exit points—three additional tunnels branching off in different directions. He knew from his memorized schematics that the leftmost passage eventually connected to the old boiler room where his extraction team would arrive. But it was also the most obvious choice.

The pursuing footsteps grew louder, echoing through the tunnel he had just traversed. Decision time.

With swift precision, the Albino removed his silk tie, draping it carefully over a valve wheel near the rightmost tunnel entrance—a false indicator of his chosen path. Then he moved silently toward the center passage, his footsteps deliberately placed to avoid creating echoes in the cavernous space.

The center tunnel was narrower, forcing him to hunch slightly as he moved forward. The walls here were older, rough-hewn stone rather than poured concrete, suggesting this section predated even the original prison construction. Water trickled down the walls, forming small rivulets along the floor. The Albino's ruined shoes splashed through these puddles, each sound causing him to wince internally.

He had progressed perhaps fifty meters when he heard voices echoing from the pumping station behind him—muted but distinguishable in the confined space.

"Split up?" A male voice, rough-edged, bearing the unmistakable accent of someone raised in the Balkans. Kovac.

"No." Female. Clipped. American, but with the flattened vowels of someone who had spent significant time in Eastern Europe. "It's what he wants."

The Albino smiled thinly despite his situation. She was good. Better than the reports had indicated. Most operatives would have divided their forces when presented with multiple escape routes, the tactical training overriding the hunter's instinct. But this woman—this Anna—thought differently. She tracked like a killer, not a soldier.

He increased his pace, the stimulant allowing him to ignore the burning in his legs and the uncomfortable racing of his heart. According to his mental map, this tunnel would eventually curve eastward, connecting with a drainage system that offered access to the old boiler room from an unexpected angle. If he could reach that junction before they determined his true path, he might still evade them long enough for extraction.

The tunnel began to slope downward, the footing becoming treacherous as the water flow increased. The Albino's hand trailed along the rough stone wall for balance, his manicured nails catching on the uneven surface: another indignity to add to the growing list.

Behind him, the sounds of pursuit had momentarily faded—they were investigating the junction.

It was time he'd managed to buy, but not much time—not much at all.

The Albino pressed himself into an alcove where ancient maintenance equipment lay forgotten, draped in decades of cobwebs and rust. The space—barely large enough for his slender frame—offered minimal concealment, but the shadows worked in his favor. Emergency lighting in this section had failed years ago, leaving only the occasional spark from deteriorating wiring to illuminate the passageway.

His fingers closed around the custom Sig Sauer P226 he'd extracted from an ankle holster. The weapon felt alien in his hand—he preferred to outsource violence rather than participate directly—but necessity had stripped away such luxuries. The pistol's weight was reassuring, its precision engineering a stark contrast to the crumbling infrastructure surrounding him.

Water trickled steadily down the curved walls, collecting in stagnant pools where concrete had cracked and subsided. Each droplet's impact resonated in the confined space—a steady backdrop to his accelerated heartbeat. The stimulant pill had fully engaged his system now, sharpening his senses to an almost painful degree. He could distinguish individual notes in the symphony of the tunnel: the distant hum of ancient generators still powering critical systems, the skittering of tiny claws as rats navigated familiar territories, the subtle shifting of settling earth above...

...and footsteps: two distinct patterns moving in methodical tandem.

The Albino checked his watch—Nine minutes until extraction. Nine minutes to survive.

"I can buy anything," he whispered to himself, the mantra settling his nerves. "I've purchased governments, militaries, revolutions. Surely I can buy nine minutes of time."

His free hand reached for the satellite phone, fingers hovering over the keys before thinking better of it. The light from the screen would betray his position, and the extraction team was already moving at maximum speed. No amount of money could bend the laws of physics to bring them faster.

Instead, he accessed the pistol's tactical light, ensuring it was disabled. Then he verified the suppressor's attachment with a practiced twist. The weapon was loaded with subsonic ammunition—specially designed rounds that would minimize the acoustic signature in these echo-prone tunnels.

He controlled his breathing, forcing his lungs to draw air in measured amounts despite the stimulant urging him toward hyperventilation. The rasping sound of his breath seemed thunderous to his chemically-enhanced hearing, each exhalation a betrayal of his position.

The footsteps grew louder: methodical, unhurried. They had the confidence of hunters who knew their game was cornered.

"He's close," a female voice murmured, the words carrying clearly through the tunnel's acoustic properties. "The water patterns are disturbed. Recent passage."

The Albino cursed silently. Of course she would notice such details.

Eight minutes. He just needed to buy eight minutes.

And if he couldn't have that... she was still only human.

A bullet would kill her as quickly as any of the men she'd cut down on her way to him. She was *human.*

"Only human," the Albino silently mouthed, nodding to himself in the dark, hand clutching his weapon.

Chapter 15

Anna moved cautiously. She could no longer hear the sound of retreating footsteps.

The Albino had evaded her three times now. He was the man who'd killed or kidnapped Beth's family—she still wasn't sure which.

He wasn't to be underestimated.

All the while, she kept an eye on Kovac. He was as dangerous—more—than the Albino. There was no telling when he might show those fangs of his and pounce on her.

But for now, the two of them moved cautiously forward, together.

Water dripped rhythmically from corroded pipes overhead, each droplet striking the shallow puddles with hypnotic precision. Anna advanced through the tunnel, her movements slick and controlled as a predator. The emergency lighting had failed in this section, leaving only the occasional spark from damaged wiring to illuminate their path. She'd switched to the night vision attachment from one of the guard's tactical helmets, the world now rendered in ghostly green phosphorescence.

The tunnel widened ahead, opening into what appeared to be an abandoned maintenance hub. Massive machinery loomed in the darkness—ancient pumps and generators from a bygone Soviet era, their metal bodies consumed by rust and time. Pipes of varying diameters snaked across the ceiling and walls, creating a metallic web that disappeared into shadowed recesses. The air hung heavy with the scent of stagnant water, mildew, and something else—a faint trace of expensive cologne that seemed jarringly out of place in these industrial catacombs.

Anna raised her fist in a silent signal, and Kovac froze behind her. She tilted her head slightly, listening beyond the ambient sounds of the tunnel system. The dripping water. The distant hum of scarcely-functioning equipment. The occasional settling of the structure above them. Nothing that indicated human movement, yet the cologne lingered, a molecular breadcrumb trail left by their quarry.

"He came this way," she whispered, her voice barely audible even in the confined space.

Kovac nodded, his single functioning eye scanning the shadows with practiced efficiency. The tactical gear he'd appropriated from the fallen guards hung on his frame like a second skin, as if he'd been born to wear such equipment.

"You've hunted him a long time," Kovac observed, his voice equally hushed. His words formed small clouds in the cool, damp air. "What did he take from you?"

Anna didn't respond immediately, her attention focused on the environmental details that might betray the Albino's hiding place. Water patterns on the concrete floor—disturbed here, indicating recent passage. Dust distributions on abandoned equipment—wiped clean in places where someone might have brushed against it. Air currents—subtly altered by the presence of another breathing body.

Kovac persisted, moving slightly closer. "A man like that collects enemies the way others collect art. But you..." His voice took on a different quality, almost appreciative. "You're different. This isn't professional. It's personal."

Anna's eyes narrowed behind the night vision goggles, catching a minute detail—a single thread caught on a jagged piece of metal. Silk, by the look of it. Expensive. She moved toward it, maintaining her tactical stance, weapon at the ready.

"Was it family?" Kovac continued, seemingly undeterred by her silence. "A lover? Or something else? I'm curious what drives someone like you to such lengths."

Anna reached the silk thread, pinching it between gloved fingers. It shimmered faintly in the green-tinted world of her night vision—a ghostly filament out of place in this forgotten underworld. She examined it briefly before tucking it into a pocket, a small piece of evidence cataloged and preserved by instinct.

"Family," she finally answered, the word escaping like the reluctant confession it was. She wasn't sure why she said it, maybe to remind herself, or perhaps out of some half-conscious tactical sense to establish connection with her temporary squad-mate. Either way, she kept her voice clinical, detached, as if discussing someone else's loss. "My sister's husband. Their daughter and son." She paused, scanning the maintenance hub with methodical precision. "I still don't know if they're alive."

Kovac absorbed this information with a slight nod, his expression unreadable in the dim light. He moved alongside her now, maintaining a precise distance—close enough for tactical coordination but far enough to react if she turned on him. His breathing had changed subtly, becoming more measured, almost meditative.

"The bonds of blood," he murmured, his voice taking on an unexpected cadence. "More binding than any chain, more compelling than any threat." His words flowed with a rhythmic quality that seemed incongruous with their surroundings and the urgency of their pursuit. "What we do for family defines us more than what we do for ourselves."

Anna cast him a sidelong glance, momentarily distracted by this shift in his demeanor. Poetry. He was reciting poetry in the middle of a manhunt, in the bowels of a maximum-security prison, while they pursued one of the most dangerous arms dealers in the world. The incongruity was jarring.

"Between the desire and the spasm," Kovac continued, his voice dropping lower as he scanned the shadows, weapon moving in perfect synchronization with his gaze, "between the potency and the existence, between the essence and the descent, falls the Shadow."

Despite herself, Anna recognized the reference. T.S. Eliot's *The Hollow Men*. It was an odd choice for a man whose violence she had witnessed firsthand on that yacht in the Mediterranean. The same man who had led a team that killed without hesitation, who had pursued her across three countries with single-minded determination. Now he quoted modernist poetry while hunting in the dark.

"Is this how you prepare?" she asked, unable to contain her curiosity despite her better judgment. "Poetry before killing?"

A ghost of a smile crossed Kovac's battered face, splitting his lip anew. A drop of blood welled, black in the night vision's monochromatic rendering. "Words have power," he replied simply. "They order chaos. They give meaning to violence." He paused, head tilting as he caught some subtle sound beyond her perception. "The universe itself began with words, did it not? 'Let there be light.' The most violent act of creation imaginable."

Anna might have dismissed this as the ramblings of a disturbed mind, but there was no denying his effectiveness. Throughout their running battle through the prison, he had moved with lethal precision.

Anna's attention snapped to where Kovac's gaze had fixed—a recessed alcove nestled between two massive pump housings. Unlike the surrounding machinery, this particular shadow seemed denser, more purposeful. The subtle wrongness of it prickled along her spine, triggering instincts honed through years of hunting and being hunted.

She approached with glacial patience, each footstep placed with deliberate care to minimize sound. The stagnant water beneath her boots might as well have been a minefield; she navigated its shallow pools by intuition, avoiding the betraying splash that would announce her advance. Her breathing slowed to near imperceptibility, her body temperature seemingly dropping to match the chill air of the tunnel system.

The alcove revealed itself gradually as she closed the distance—a maintenance nook carved into the concrete wall, perhaps originally intended to house electrical equipment or emergency supplies. Decades of neglect had transformed it into a perfect hiding place, its entrance partially obscured by the hulking silhouette of a decommissioned transformer. Rust had frozen its metal door half-open, creating a narrow gap just wide enough for a slender man to slip through.

Something glinted at the edge of her night vision—a momentary reflection that vanished as quickly as it appeared. Not water. Something smoother, more deliberate: metal, polished metal.

She froze, her body becoming statue-still. Behind her, Kovac had also stopped, reading her body language with the intuitive understanding of a fellow predator. Neither spoke. Neither needed to.

The air in the tunnel seemed to thicken, molecules arranging themselves into layers of tension. Even the water droplets appeared to slow their descent, as if the entire underground world held its breath in anticipation of violence.

Anna's enhanced vision detected the subtlest disturbance in the air flowing from the alcove—a rhythm that didn't match the tunnel's natural ventilation patterns. It was breathing... controlled, measured, but unmistakably human. The Albino was trying to regulate his respiration, to become invisible through stillness, but the betraying cadence of life couldn't be fully suppressed.

Her finger hovered near the trigger of her weapon, not touching it yet, maintaining that crucial fragment of decision space between thought and action. She calculated angles, visualizing the confined space beyond the rusted door, constructing a three-dimensional model in her mind. If he was pressed against the left wall, she would need to adjust her entry angle by approximately twenty degrees. If he had wedged himself into the far corner, the initial shot would need to be lower, accounting for his likely crouched position.

Kovac had positioned himself at her three o'clock, establishing a crossfire position without needing to be directed. Despite their mutual enmity, their tactical synchronization was flawless—strangers who had danced this same ballet many times.

A bead of condensation formed on a pipe above the alcove, swelling with glacial patience until gravity claimed it. It fell, striking the metal door.

It was like a starter's pistol.

The Albino emerged, firing twice.

Anna spotted the gun a split-second before the bullets came. She flung herself, instincts taking over—protect the team. Her training acted for her.

Protect the team.

Protect the—

She slammed into Kovac, sending them both sprawling as bullets sparked off the pipes behind where their torsos would have been.

The two of them hit the ground in a tangle.

The Albino cursed, ducking behind a pipe of his own.

Now that he'd missed his surprise attack, he shouted, his voice strong despite the evident fear in his eyes peeking over the rusted pipe.

"You can't trust her, Kovac!" he shouted. "She's a killer. She'll use you then execute you!"

Kovac extricated himself from where Anna had tackled him. He moved like a pool of shadow, spilling across the floor in an almost scuttling motion before rising behind a concrete pillar as if his legs were still cords.

The Albino's voice echoed through the chamber, bouncing off rusted machinery and concrete walls. "She's hunting me because I have what she wants! Information! About her family!"

Anna's body tensed, the words striking deeper than any bullet could have. Her finger tightened imperceptibly on her trigger, muscle memory warring with the desperate need to keep this man alive for questioning.

Kovac glanced at her, his single functioning eye assessing her reaction with clinical detachment. The tactical synchronization that had carried them this far suddenly felt fragile, a temporary alliance that could shatter at any moment.

"Your sister's husband is still alive," the Albino called out, his voice taking on a silky quality that seemed to slither through the darkness. "The children too. For now."

Anna remained motionless, only her eyes moving as she tracked the source of his voice. He was shifting position, using the acoustics of the chamber to mask his true location. Amateur mistake—speaking gave away more than it concealed.

"He's lying," she said quietly to Kovac, her voice flat and controlled despite the storm raging beneath her professional exterior. "It's what he does."

The Albino laughed, the sound unnaturally high-pitched in the cavernous space. "Am I? Ask yourself why I would keep them alive, Anna. Assets. Leverage. Insurance." A pause, punctuated by the metallic click of a magazine being changed. "You kill me, you never find them. That's why you haven't pulled the trigger yet, isn't it? Why you've been hunting me instead of executing me from a distance."

"I can still change my mind on that," Anna replied, her voice carrying just enough to reach him without revealing her exact position. "For the moment, I need you alive."

"And I need you reasonable, not vengeful," the Albino countered. "We're both professionals. We both understand transaction." Water splashed as he moved again, circling toward the far side of the chamber. "I can give you what you want. Coordinates. Proof of life. In exchange for safe passage."

Kovac shifted slightly, adjusting his position to maintain the tactical advantage. His movements were precise, economical, almost beautiful in their lethal efficiency. "He's stalling," he murmured, his voice barely audible even to Anna. "Extraction team incoming."

Anna nodded once, acknowledging both the tactical assessment and the unspoken question hanging between them. Did she want the Albino dead or alive? Could she trust herself to make that decision objectively?

"Where are they?" she called out, injecting a note of desperate hope into her voice—an allowed vulnerability to keep him talking while she maneuvered closer.

"Only one man knows. The one I sold them to!" The words broke off in a laugh.

Anna hesitated. She still wasn't sure she believed him. "Who?" she demanded.

"Funnily, I am going to meet him. Tomorrow. You can come with me. Ask him yourself."

She paused, considering this.

The Albino's words hung in the stagnant air, seductive in their promise, poisonous in their intent. Anna felt the familiar coldness spreading through her chest—the detachment that had kept her alive through a hundred operations, a thousand moments when emotion threatened to override judgment.

"Proof," she said, her voice hardening to flint. "Now. Not tomorrow. Not at some meeting. Here."

Water sloshed faintly as the Albino shifted position again. "Such impatience," he chided, his cultured voice echoing off the curved walls. "That's always been your weakness, hasn't it? The Gabriel temper. Your sister had it too—that flash in her eyes when she realized what was happening. When her husband tried to intervene." A soft chuckle. "Admirable, but ultimately futile."

Anna's grip tightened on her weapon, the pressure threatening to warp the composite frame. The image his words conjured—Beth's face contorted in fear and rage, her husband stepping forward to protect his family—sliced through her professional detachment like a scalpel. She forced her breathing to remain steady, refusing to give him the satisfaction of an emotional response.

"You're describing a standard home invasion," she replied, voice clinically cold. "Nothing that proves they're alive. Nothing that couldn't be gleaned from police reports or witness statements."

She was moving as she spoke, each word carefully timed to mask the sound of her boots in the shallow water. Three meters to the left, two forward, using a massive valve housing as cover. The night vision rendered the Albino's hiding spot in ghostly green phosphorescence—his outline barely visible behind a junction of pipes, the faint heat signature of his body betraying his position despite his attempts at concealment.

"The boy has a birthmark," the Albino said suddenly, his voice dropping to a near-whisper that nonetheless carried in the acoustic chamber. "Left shoulder blade. Shaped like the continent of Africa. The girl told me about her bedroom—she collects elephant figurines—twenty-three of them on a shelf above her bed. The smallest is carved from jade, a gift from her grandfather before he died."

Anna's blood froze in her veins. The birthmark. The elephant collection. These were details too specific to be fabricated, too personal to be gathered from surveillance alone. Her mind raced through possibilities—had he been in their home before the abduction? Of course he had. Did he remember? Or had he spoken to them *after* the abduction. Were they really still alive?

"The jade elephant was from her grandmother," she corrected, the words escaping before she could stop them. A test. A desperate attempt to catch him in a lie.

"No," the Albino replied with quiet certainty. "It was from William Gabriel. Your father's father. Given to her on her fifth birthday, three weeks before his heart attack. She keeps it separated from the others because it's 'special'."

Anna let out a breath. "Are they still together? All three of them?"

"Processing!" he called back. "Preparing. The man I sold them too... he's patient with his commodities. Wants maximum value."

"They're children," Anna snapped. "What about their father? Is he still alive?"

A scornful snort. "Don't be naive. What use would I have for an adult male? An *American.* They can't be trained. They're feral. He's dead, and you know it."

Anna had suspected as much. On the illicit market, an American man would entail a lot of risk.

The Albino's admission struck Anna with physical force, confirming the grim suspicion she'd carried since the beginning. Her brother-in-law, who taught history at the university, who collected vintage vinyl records, who made terrible puns that made Beth simultaneously groan and smile—gone. But the children—her niece and nephew—might still be alive.

"Tomorrow's meeting," she said, voice steady despite the grief and rage swirling beneath. "Who's the buyer?"

"That information is worth considerably more than my temporary cooperation," the Albino replied, his tone shifting to something almost business-like. "It's my only leverage. My insurance policy." He shifted slightly, water rippling around his expensive shoes. "But I can offer you a gesture of good faith. The facility where they were initially processed. Security protocols. Guard rotations."

The Albino was approximately seven meters away, partially shielded by a complex junction of pipes and valves. Kovac had maintained his position on her right flank, establishing a perfect crossfire scenario. They could take him now—wound him, not kill him—and extract the information through less diplomatic means.

As if reading her thoughts, the Albino added, "I've taken precautions, of course." Then he emerged from behind the pipes, smiling.

His tongue jutted out. He held out his arms as if he were on a crucifix and jammed out his tongue.

On that tongue sat a small blue pill.

Chapter 16

Anna stared, mind processing. The blue pill was something she recognized. The sort of thing Nazi officers had often hidden in their teeth in case they were captured.

The blue pill gleamed with artificial brightness on the Albino's extended tongue, a silent warning hovering between life and death: a suicide capsule, a final escape route that would render all Anna's careful hunting meaningless.

"Insurance," the Albino articulated carefully around the pill, his colorless eyes never leaving Anna's face. "One bite, and whatever information I possess about your sister's children dies with me." He smiled thinly, the expression never reaching those pale eyes. "Shall we negotiate like civilized people now?"

Anna held herself perfectly still, weapon trained on him but finger deliberately outside the trigger guard. The scenario had shifted dramatically—no longer a simple capture mission but a psychological standoff where the slightest miscalculation could cost her everything.

"What do you want?" she asked, voice level, professional.

The Albino slowly closed his mouth, the pill disappearing but clearly held ready between his teeth. "Safe passage," he replied, his articulation deliberately precise. "Your escort to my extraction point. After which, I provide coordinates to the processing facility where your niece and nephew were taken."

"And the buyer?" Anna pressed. "The one you're meeting tomorrow?"

"That," the Albino said, "remains my insurance for a later transaction. One negotiation at a time. He did buy them, though. He has... a fondness for children—sees them as an expensive commodity. Everyone has a price."

Kovac shifted slightly to Anna's right, maintaining his firing position but adjusting his stance. His expression remained unreadable, but something in his posture had changed—a coiling of potential energy, like a spring compressing.

"You're in no position to dictate terms," Kovac said suddenly, his voice carrying the casual menace of a jaguar toying with wounded prey. "That pill won't save you from pain. Only from answers."

The Albino's gaze flickered to Kovac, a flash of genuine fear crossing his features before his professional mask reasserted itself. "The former Spetsnaz operative," he acknowledged with a slight nod. "I've read your file. Impressive work in Grozny. Less so in Ankara." His thin lips curved in a smile that didn't reach his eyes. "Did they put you in the cell next to mine as a joke, I wonder? Two of Anna Gabriel's most dedicated enemies, separated by a concrete wall."

Kovac didn't respond to the provocation, his single functioning eye remaining fixed on the Albino with predatory focus. The stillness of his body spoke of complete control—a man who had mastered the art of waiting for the perfect moment to strike.

"Enough," Anna cut in, reclaiming control of the negotiation. "You want extraction. I want information. Let's establish terms."

The Albino nodded, visibly relaxing as the conversation returned to transactional territory he understood. "My team is three minutes out," he said, checking his watch with deliberate casualness. "They'll arrive at the old boiler room, northeast quadrant of the facility..."

"And this man you sold them too," Anna said quietly, "You intend to meet him tomorrow?"

A faint nod. "You'll have no idea where. No clue *who*. You can't do this without me."

Anna considered this, calm, rational.

"Prove to me you sold them," she said quietly. "Prove it. Now."

He stared at her.

"Do it," she aimed her gun at his forehead.

He was sweating. He swallowed, careful to keep the pill pinched between his teeth, unbroken.

He turned to Kovac. "She's your target, isn't she? I thought you never let a target slip away."

Kovac grinned and quoted another poem, "The woods are lovely, dark and deep," Kovac recited, his voice taking on that strange lyrical quality again. "But I have promises to keep, and miles to go before I sleep."

The Albino's eyes narrowed at the poetry, clearly unsettled by Kovac's unpredictable response. He turned back to Anna, calculation evident in his gaze.

"You want proof?" he asked, reaching slowly into his jacket pocket. "I have something. A screenshot of the money paid. The product listed."

"Product?" she asked, her voice cold.

He flashed a smile, nodding. "Tony? Was it. Five years old? Sarah just had her fourth birthday."

Anna felt her skin crawl as he spoke.

Anna's finger twitched against the trigger guard, a minute movement that only Kovac—with his predator's attention to detail—would have noticed. The casual way the Albino spoke her niece and nephew's names sent ice through her veins, crystallizing her rage into something cold and precise.

"Show me," she commanded, voice stripped of emotion.

The Albino withdrew a sleek satellite phone from his pocket, movements deliberately slow to avoid provoking a shot. His bone-white fingers swiped across the screen with practiced efficiency, navigating through layers of encryption before turning the display toward Anna.

"See for yourself," he said, holding the phone at arm's length. "The transaction record. Two million euros each. Premium merchandise."

Anna stepped forward cautiously, her weapon never wavering from its target position between the Albino's eyes. The screen displayed what appeared to be a financial ledger—cryptocurrency transactions, routing numbers, alphanumeric codes that meant nothing to her. But below that, unmistakable: two entries labeled simply "S.G. (F/4)" and "T.G. (M/5)" followed by payment confirmations.

Sarah Gabriel. Tony Gabriel. Beth had kept her family name—a sign of respect. Female, four years old. Male, five years old.

"Where?" Anna demanded, her voice dropping to a dangerous whisper.

The Albino smiled thinly, pulling the phone back. "That information comes after my extraction. As I said, one transaction at a time."

Kovac had shifted position again, moving silently to establish a better angle. Water rippled around his boots as he settled into his new stance.

"Three minutes," the Albino reminded them, glancing at his watch again. "My team will not negotiate. They have standing orders to eliminate any threats upon arrival." He looked pointedly at Anna. "Even if that means sacrificing potentially valuable intelligence."

Anna didn't reply—didn't speak.

She'd already made up her mind after all.

"Thank you," she said simply. "For unlocking your phone."

Then she shot him in the wrist. He howled in pain, his phone falling. She reached out to snatch it. At the same time, she shot him in the knee.

The Albino growled in pain. He fell to the ground, the pill still in his teeth.

She stood over him, watching him bleed. She didn't speak now, didn't quite remember *how*. When this mindset came over her, she forgot the use of words entirely.

He was blubbering, pleading.

She shot him in the other leg—then in the arm.

Anna watched the crimson bloom spread across the Albino's pristine white shirt, clutching desperately at the wound as if trying to push life back into his failing body. His colorless eyes, once cold and lethal, now flickered with something primal—fear, perhaps, or simply the animal recognition of approaching death. The concrete floor beneath him darkened with each labored heartbeat, blood pooling in a slick, expanding circle.

She could finish him now. One clean shot. A mercy he didn't deserve.

Instead, Anna crouched beside him, her movements deliberate, almost tender. The Albino's breath came in wet, rattling gasps as she studied his phone he'd unlocked for her. She'd have to make sure the screen remained on. The arrogance of a man who never expected to be caught, who believed his security lay in human shields.

"The children," she whispered, her voice like gravel. "Where are they being kept?"

The Albino's lips twitched, a ghost of his earlier smirk. "Insurance... policy," he managed, blood bubbling at the corner of his mouth. "You'll never... find them... without..."

The first additional shot took him in the thigh, precise and controlled. Not immediately fatal, but enough to accelerate the inevitable. The Albino's scream echoed through the empty corridors of the abandoned prison block, bouncing off concrete and steel like a living thing.

"Wrong answer," Anna said, her face impassive as she checked the phone's screen. Satellite tracking disabled. Smart. But the message history remained.

The second shot pierced his shoulder, deliberately missing the artery. The Albino's body convulsed, his designer shoes scraping uselessly against the floor, leaving crimson smears like macabre artwork.

"They're children," Anna said, standing now, looking down at the dying man. "My sister's children."

Blood loss would take him within twenty minutes. It would be painful... and slow, exactly what he deserved. Anna held the phone away from her body. Keeping it on. He'd shown her the transaction. He'd claimed he had a meeting.

She didn't need him.

No. More than that. She couldn't abide him breathing another day. Some things just *had* to be. His death was one such thing.

Behind her, the Albino's breathing grew more labored, a countdown clock of wet, strangled gasps.

She noticed the blue pill had fallen from his slack lips.

With a disgusted snort, she reached down and plucked his gun from where he was reaching for it and flung it far away.

Then she picked up the dusty pill, gently placing it back on his tongue. Her hand trailed his cheek almost gently. "Coward," she whispered. "I knew you wouldn't."

She then stood to her feet. She didn't look back, her boots leaving bloody prints that grew fainter with each step as she stalked away down the corridor.

GUARDIAN'S MISSION

One minute until his extraction team arrived.

Chapter 17

Kovac watched Anna as the two of them moved towards the glowing moonlight. They'd shot the lock to the service door and now slowly emerged from the dark into the damp night air like specters leaving their mausoleum.

He hadn't anticipated *any* of that.

Slowly, the mercenary was realizing that the American may even be crazier than he was. And as she led the way, he just stared at her, stunned and smiling.

She'd saved his life from those bullets, a strange equalizing of debt. He never let a target go. But he never failed to repay a debt. And the dilemma created an odd quandary for sure.

He caught her arm as she began to climb up the service ladder, and she looked down at him in tense appraisal. She kept the

Albino's phone in one hand, extended ahead of her. She had been reading the messages, scanning the outgoing calls.

"You killed him?"

"He's probably still bleeding," she replied, not really confirming or denying.

"He will die, though," Kovac replied. Usually he was not one to quibble over such details, but the American had put him off balance.

His hand still gripping her arm while she held the ladder with one hand, the phone with the other, she stared down at him as if she were taking a moment to translate his words, though he had spoken plain English for her ease. Her eyes were dark, unblinking. For a moment, it was as if all light had vanished.

"Yes," she said simply. "He *will* die."

It was a simple fact, no question in the words at all. They both knew it.

Anna continued her ascent up the service ladder, the rusted metal warm beneath her free hand despite the chill underground. Kovac followed, his movements fluid despite his injuries. The Albino's phone cast a blue-white glow across her face as she scanned through messages, contacts, and calendar entries—information more precious than gold.

Moonlight spilled through the opening above, a silver beacon guiding them toward freedom. The distant wail of sirens suggested the prison remained in chaos, attention focused on the riot of released isolation prisoners and those from the yard that were still at large. With the warden and the response team dead, it was difficult to say how much attention the two escapees emerging from a forgotten maintenance shaft half a kilometer from the main facility would receive.

They reached the surface, emerging into a small equipment yard surrounded by a chain-link fence topped with razor wire. Beyond lay dense forest, dark and inviting in its promise of concealment. The night air felt shockingly fresh after the stagnant tunnels, carrying the scent of pine and recent rain.

Anna moved immediately toward the fence, assessing weak points, mentally computing the fastest route to disappear into the wilderness beyond. Kovac followed more slowly, his medical training automatically cataloging the Albino's injuries in his mind.

"Four gunshot wounds," he said quietly, his voice carrying in the still night air. "The first to the wrist—radius fractured, ulnar artery likely severed. Significant blood loss, but not immediately fatal with pressure. Second to the knee—patellar destruction, femoral involvement probable but you deliberately avoided the artery. Third shot to the opposite thigh—similar damage, again avoiding major vessels. Final shot to the shoulder—trapezius muscle destroyed, scapula shattered, subclavian artery missed by approximately two centimeters."

He paused, his single functioning eye studying Anna's silhouette against the moonlight. "Precisely calculated to maximize pain while extending consciousness. Significant blood loss, but death would take between fifteen and twenty-two minutes depending on his heart rate and blood pressure. Long enough to experience the full progression of hypovolemic shock—anxiety giving way to confusion, then weakness, then the cold certainty of approaching death."

Anna didn't respond, her attention fixed on the phone's screen as she scrolled through the Albino's communications, hunting for anything that might lead to her niece and nephew.

"You've done this before," Kovac observed, neither accusation nor admiration coloring his words—simply professional assessment.

When she remained silent, he pressed further, genuine curiosity evident in his voice. "Why not a clean kill? A professional like you could have placed a bullet between his eyes in less than a second. Why extend his suffering?"

Anna looked up from the phone once more, her eyes meeting his. The moonlight revealed nothing in her expression—no satisfaction, no remorse, no anger. Just the empty calm of someone who had crossed a line so many times it no longer registered as a boundary.

"He sold children," she said simply, as if this explained everything.

"Many have committed worse crimes," Kovac replied with a shrug.

She looked at him, her studying look turning a shade more curious. "Are you still hunting me?" she asked.

He considered this as well. Though, he'd put off the question, it was still a debate that demanded an answer. Kovac licked his lips. "I need to hunt," he replied noncommittally.

"Two million for each of Beth's children. Four million in total. If we find the man who bought them, you can keep his money."

Kovac blinked as the words hit him, a second later he smirked. "Are you offering me a job?"

Anna gave a slow resolute nod. But before he could reply, she suddenly held up a finger to her lips. Ahead was the sound of an approaching helicopter. Flashlights shone through the dark trees.

The extraction team had arrived.

Anna assessed, paused then gestured to the left. A clear path. Kovac had spotted it too.

The two of them moved like lethal shadows through the forest, each step precisely placed to minimize sound. The helicopter's searchlight swept the clearing behind them, its powerful beam cutting through darkness like a knife. Voices carried on the night air—tense, professional, speaking in clipped Russian military jargon.

Kovac murmured, his voice barely audible above the helicopter's thrum. "They'll pursue once they secure the body."

Anna nodded as she navigated through the dense undergrowth. The Albino's phone remained clutched in her hand, its screen now dark to avoid betraying their position. She'd likely already committed the critical information to memory—coordinates, contact protocols, meeting locations.

"Two kilometers east," she said, orienting herself by the stars visible through breaks in the forest canopy. "I have a vehicle."

Kovac raised an eyebrow but didn't question how she'd arranged extraction from a maximum-security prison in remote Russia. Instead, he adjusted his course to match hers.

The helicopter's searchlight swept closer, its beam illuminating patches of forest floor mere meters from where they crouched behind a fallen pine. The extraction team was methodical, professional—expanding their search pattern in concentric circles from the maintenance shaft exit.

"We need a diversion," Anna whispered, eyes scanning their surroundings for options.

Without hesitation, Kovac removed a grenade from his tactical vest—one of several he'd collected from the fallen prison guards. "How far is your vehicle?"

"Twenty minutes at this pace."

He nodded once, a decision made. "I'll draw them northeast. Circle back and meet you at the vehicle." He paused, studying her face in the diffused moonlight.

"Does that mean you'll take the job?" she asked.

His blind eye crinkled as his lip ticked up in a smirk, and he answered in a silent nod.

"The Albino said he had a meeting tomorrow," Anna said. She wriggled the phone. "And I know the phone number of who he was going to meet."

"You're sure?"

She scowled. "I'm positive."

"Who?"

"A war hero. A famous figure named Anthony Starr. A man supposed to be dead. A four-star US general said to have died three years ago." She held up the phone, showing Kovac the most recent message thread. The name glowed in the darkness, impossible yet undeniable.

Kovac whistled softly, the sound barely audible above the distant helicopter's thrum. "Didn't he run a private security firm? I remember their name. Some of the best in the business." His lips twisted into a sardonic smile. "They wouldn't hire me. Psych eval."

Anna's face remained impassive, but her eyes had taken on a new intensity as she tucked the phone securely into her tactical vest.

"Starr Private Solutions," she confirmed. "Government contracts worth billions. Military training programs in thirty-seven countries. Specialized in 'high-value asset protection' and 'extraction services.'" Her voice took on a bitter edge at the euphemisms. "Perfect cover for *other* activities."

The helicopter's searchlight swept closer, forcing them deeper into the shadow of a massive pine. Kovac's fingers danced over the grenade's surface, checking the pin, weighing it with the casual familiarity of someone who had deployed such devices countless times.

"I encountered his teams twice," he murmured, eyes tracking the search pattern above them. "Once in Ankara, once in Lviv. Military precision. Absolute discipline. No survivors unless they intended it." He glanced at Anna, something like respect flickering across his battered features. "You must have impressed him if he kept your family alive."

Anna's jaw tightened almost imperceptibly. "Or they're valuable to him in some other way."

Kovac nodded, understanding without further explanation. Children with connections to intelligence operatives were potential goldmines—leverage, information sources, potential recruits for future operations. The black market valued them accordingly.

"If Starr is alive," he said, voice dropping lower as the helicopter passed overhead, "then whatever operation he's running goes beyond standard human trafficking. A man with his connections, his resources..." He trailed off, implications hanging in the night air between them.

"I know," Anna replied, her voice hardening to steel. "Which is why I'm going to find him, and I'm going to make him tell me where my sister's children are." She paused, eyes meeting Kovac's in the darkness. "Even if I have to dismantle everything he's built piece by piece."

Kovac's undamaged eye gleamed with something between amusement and appreciation. "Starting with his meeting tomorrow." It wasn't a question.

Anna nodded once, a sharp, decisive movement. "Now... distraction. Ready? Reconvene at the coordinates here. Memorize."

She flashed him the phone. He blinked and gave a subtle jut of his chin in confirmation.

Then he pulled the grenade pin.

Chapter 18

Anna approached the idling vehicle, feeling a slow well of relief as she recognized the single figure in the driver's seat. Casper's silhouette was unmistakable even in the pre-dawn darkness—the military-straight posture, the distinctive shape of his shaved head, the patient stillness of a man who had mastered the art of waiting. The dark SUV was positioned perfectly, half-hidden beneath the spreading branches of ancient pines, its engine purring with barely audible efficiency. Just as they had planned.

She emerged from the treeline cautiously, senses still heightened from the prison escape. Her tactical gear was filthy, streaked with tunnel grime, rust stains, and darker patches she knew to be blood—both others' and her own. The Albino's satellite phone remained clutched in her left hand, knuckles white with the force of her grip. Its screen glowed faintly, illuminating the exhaustion etched into her face.

GUARDIAN'S MISSION

Casper spotted her immediately, his head turning with the precision of a radar dish locking onto a signal. For a moment, he remained motionless, as if processing the visual confirmation against expected parameters. Then something extraordinary happened—something Anna had witnessed perhaps twice in their decade-long partnership.

Casper's professional mask shattered.

He erupted from the driver's seat, door flung wide with uncharacteristic abandon. The man who had maintained perfect composure during firefights in Kandahar, who had calmly applied a tourniquet to his own leg while under sniper fire in Mosul, who had never once broken protocol during their most desperate operations—that man was suddenly gone, replaced by someone driven purely by emotion.

"Anna!" His voice cracked on her name, the single word carrying a universe of relief and concern. He crossed the distance between them in four long strides, his movements lacking their usual calculated efficiency.

Before she could respond, his arms enveloped her in an embrace so fierce it momentarily lifted her from the ground. The unexpected contact triggered her combat reflexes for a split second before her brain registered: Casper. Safety. Home.

"Holy shit," he whispered into her hair, his usually steady voice trembling slightly. "When the alarms started... when the radio chatter indicated a full facility lockdown... I thought—" He didn't finish the sentence, couldn't articulate the fear that had gripped him during those interminable hours of waiting.

Anna found herself returning the embrace with equal intensity, her face pressed against the familiar scent of his tactical jacket—gun oil, mint chewing gum, and that particular brand of soap he'd used since their SEAL days. Her body suddenly remembered all the pain and exhaustion she'd been suppressing, and she sagged slightly against his solid frame.

"I got him," she murmured, the words muffled against his chest. "The Albino. He's dead."

Casper pulled back just enough to study her face, his hands still gripping her shoulders as if afraid she might vanish. His eyes—sharp, assessing, trained to miss nothing—cataloged her injuries, the blood staining her clothing, the hollowed exhaustion beneath her determined expression.

"And Beth's kids?" he asked softly, knowing the question that had driven her across three continents, through firefights and interrogations, into the heart of a Russian maximum-security prison.

Anna held up the Albino's phone. "Leads. Real ones this time. He sold them to Anthony Starr."

Casper's eyebrows shot up, professional composure reasserting itself at the mention of that name. "Starr? The general? He's been dead for—"

"Three years," Anna finished. "Apparently not." She gestured toward the SUV. "We need to move. I have a meeting to prepare for."

Casper hesitated, eyes scanning the tree-line behind her. "You said 'we' earlier on the radio. Who—"

The question died in his throat as a figure emerged from the forest with ghost-like silence. Kovac moved with hawk-like grace despite his injuries, tactical gear gleaming dully in the pre-dawn light. His battered face remained expressionless as he approached, a stolen assault rifle held casually across his chest.

Casper's reaction was instantaneous. He shoved Anna behind him with one arm while the other drew his sidearm in a movement too fast to track. The weapon leveled at Kovac's head, rock-steady despite the adrenaline that must have flooded his system.

"Anna," Casper said, voice deadly quiet, never taking his eyes off Kovac. "Please explain why the man who tried to kill us in Turkmenistan is walking toward our extraction vehicle."

Kovac stopped, making no move toward his own weapon. His single functioning eye regarded Casper with clinical interest, like a biologist observing a particularly fascinating specimen. His lips curved into something approximating a smile.

"You must be Casper," he said, voice rasping slightly from his prison beatings. "She mentioned you. Former SEAL. Close-quarters combat specialist. Impressive record in Afghanistan." His head tilted slightly. "You favor your right side. Old injury to the left knee, perhaps? Something that healed well enough for field work but still affects your weight distribution under stress."

Casper's expression remained impassive, but Anna could read the minute tensing of his shoulders that indicated Kovac's assessment had hit uncomfortably close to home.

"Anna," Casper repeated, finger steady on the trigger. "Explanation. Now."

She moved to stand beside him rather than behind him—a subtle but significant repositioning that communicated volumes to her former teammate. "Temporary alliance," she said, voice calm and measured. "He was in the cell next to the Albino. Helped me escape." She paused, eyes meeting Casper's. "And he knows things about Starr's operation that we need."

Casper's weapon remained trained on Kovac, unwavering despite the new information. "The same Kovac who led a tactical team onto that yacht in the Mediterranean? Who killed the captain and three crew members? Who chased us across three countries trying to put bullets in our heads?"

Kovac's damaged face twisted into what might have been a smile. "You forgot Bucharest," he said mildly. "The café bombing. That was one of mine as well."

"Not helping your case," Anna muttered, stepping fully between the two men. Her eyes locked with Casper's, communicating volumes in the silent language they'd developed through years of operations together. *Trust me. I know what I'm doing.*

"He's a contract killer, Anna," Casper said, voice dropping to a dangerous whisper. "A sadist who quotes poetry to his victims before executing them."

"T.S. Eliot, primarily," Kovac interjected, seemingly unperturbed by the gun aimed at his head. "Though I've been exploring Frost recently. There's something about his meter that complements the rhythm of close-quarters combat."

Anna watched a muscle twitch in Casper's jaw—a tell she recognized from countless high-stress situations.

"Beth's kids," she said quietly, knowing those two words would cut through his professional caution more effectively than any tactical argument. "Starr has them. Kovac has crossed paths with Starr's organization before. He knows their operational patterns, their security protocols." She paused, letting the implications sink in. "And he's agreed to help."

Casper's eyes flicked briefly to her face, then back to Kovac. "Why?" he demanded. "What's your angle?"

Kovac shrugged, the movement oddly elegant despite his battered appearance. "Professional curiosity, perhaps. Or maybe I'm simply intrigued by the opportunity to observe Anna Gabriel at closer range." His undamaged eye gleamed with something unreadable in the pre-dawn light. "She kills beautifully."

The statement hung in the air between them, charged with implications none of them were prepared to address. Casper's finger tightened imperceptibly on the trigger.

"Four million," Anna cut in, her voice sharp enough to break the dangerous tension building between the men. "The buyer paid two million each for the children. When we find them, Kovac gets whatever funds we recover from Starr's operation." She met Casper's incredulous gaze steadily. "That's the deal."

Casper's expression shifted subtly—surprise giving way to appraisal. "You're paying him to help rescue your family?"

"I'm leveraging his expertise," Anna corrected. "And providing financial motivation to ensure his cooperation."

Kovac nodded, his single functioning eye glittering with something approaching amusement. "She's also betting that my professional curiosity will keep me from killing her until after we've found the children," he added conversationally, as if discussing the weather rather than potential homicide. "A reasonable calculation. I've always preferred to complete the current contract before pursuing personal interests."

The statement hung in the pre-dawn air, neither threat nor reassurance but something unsettlingly between. Casper's weapon remained steady, his eyes never leaving Kovac's face as he processed the implications of Anna's decision. The forest around them had fallen into that peculiar hush that precedes sunrise—birds not yet singing, nocturnal creatures already returned to their dens, the world suspended between night and day.

"This is insane," Casper finally said, his voice low and controlled.

Anna held his gaze steadily. "Yes."

Casper exhaled slowly, a carefully measured release of breath that did nothing to diminish the dangerous energy radiating from him. His tactical vest rose and fell with the deliberate rhythm of someone using breathing techniques to manage combat stress. The scar that bisected his left eyebrow—a souvenir from their joint operation in Kandahar—seemed more pronounced in the harsh angles of the SUV's headlights.

"The trunk," he said finally, the words clipped and non-negotiable. "He rides in the trunk."

Kovac's battered face remained impassive, but something like amusement flickered in his undamaged eye. The night dew had settled on his stolen tactical gear, tiny droplets catching the first hint of dawn light filtering through the pine branches overhead. Despite his injuries—the swollen eye, split lip, likely broken ribs—he maintained the poised stillness of a predator at rest.

"The trunk," Casper repeated, emphasizing each syllable as if speaking to someone with limited comprehension. "Or he finds his own extraction." His finger hadn't moved from the trigger, the barrel of his weapon unwavering in its focus on the center of Kovac's forehead.

Anna glanced between the two men, observing the delicate balance of this fragile alliance. It didn't have to last forever... just long enough. The extraction point would remain secure for only twenty more minutes at most before Russian authorities expanded their search perimeter to include this sector. They needed to move, and soon.

Kovac snorted, the sound incongruously normal coming from a man whose reputation inspired whispered warnings in intelligence communities across three continents. "Your partner lacks imagination," he observed, his voice carrying that strange poetic cadence that seemed to emerge when he was amused.

Kovac considered this ultimatum, his head tilting slightly as if weighing the relative merits of dignity versus practicality. The first golden rays of dawn filtered through the pine canopy, casting dappled patterns across his battered face and illuminating the dried blood that had crusted along his jawline. A bird called somewhere in the distance—the first tentative notes of the forest awakening from its nocturnal silence.

"The trunk," Casper repeated, every muscle in his body coiled with the potential for violence. The weapon in his hand might as well have been an extension of his arm, so naturally did it align with Kovac's forehead. Morning mist curled around his boots, ghostly tendrils dissipating with each subtle shift of his weight.

Anna remained between them, her exhaustion momentarily forgotten as she weighed the probability of this standoff escalating into bloodshed. The tactical dynamics were familiar to her—two apex predators establishing dominance, neither willing to show weakness. She had seen such confrontations in Afghanistan, in the mountain passes where tribal warlords measured each other with similar deadly intensity.

Kovac snorted, the sound unexpectedly human coming from someone who had demonstrated such inhuman capacity for violence. "The trunk," he echoed, his voice carrying the slightest trace of amusement beneath its raspy texture. "How... American." He gestured toward the vehicle with a casual sweep of his hand, the movement deliberately slow to avoid triggering Casper's combat reflexes. "Perhaps we could compromise? The backseat, with restraints of your choosing?"

Casper's jaw tightened, the minuscule movement visible only to someone who knew him as well as Anna did. The scar along his eyebrow seemed to whiten slightly as blood vessels constricted beneath the skin—a physiological tell she had observed during particularly stressful operations.

"This isn't a negotiation," Casper replied, each word precise and final. "Trunk. Secured. Or you find your own way out of a maximum-security prison zone during active manhunt operations." His eyes narrowed fractionally. "Your injuries suggest you've already received significant attention from the prison guards. I imagine a second encounter would be... educational."

The air between them seemed to crystallize with tension, molecules arranging themselves into patterns of potential violence. Anna could almost taste the metallic tang of adrenaline on her tongue, her own body preparing instinctively for the possibility of sudden movement, of bullets, of blood.

Kovac shrugged, the gesture oddly elegant despite his tactical gear and injuries. "Very well," he conceded, as if granting a minor favor rather than accepting non-negotiable terms. "The trunk." His undamaged eye swept over the SUV, assessing its dimensions.

He didn't seem bothered by the indignity of the arrangement, his acceptance coming with the casual ease of someone accustomed to difficult situations.

The morning mist parted as they approached the SUV, tendrils of vapor swirling around their boots like spectral fingers grasping at their ankles. Casper maintained his firing position as Anna opened the vehicle's rear compartment, the hydraulic lifts hissing softly in the pre-dawn stillness. The cargo area was surprisingly spacious—a custom modification that spoke of previous operations requiring discreet transportation. A tactical mesh divider separated it from the main cabin, reinforced with carbon fiber struts that would withstand significant impact.

"Comfortable?" Anna asked, her voice betraying nothing as Kovac assessed his temporary prison.

"I've endured worse accommodations," he replied, eyeing the space with clinical detachment. "Though perhaps with better company."

Without warning, Kovac moved—an almost balletic shift of weight that brought him to the edge of the trunk. Casper's weapon tracked him with mechanical precision, but Kovac made no aggressive motion. Instead, he lowered himself into the compartment, arranging his battered body with the careful economy of someone accustomed to confined spaces. His single functioning eye gleamed in the shadows, reflecting the first rays of dawn light filtering through the trees.

"The Albino underestimated you," he observed, looking up at Anna as she prepared to close the hatch. "A common mistake when dealing with the Guardian Angel, I suspect."

Anna paused, her hand on the trunk lid. Something flickered across her face—a microexpression too brief to interpret. "Yes," she replied simply. "It was."

The trunk closed with a definitive thunk, sealing Kovac in darkness. Casper maintained his vigilance until the electronic locks engaged, their mechanical chirp confirming the compartment was secure. Only then did he lower his weapon, the tension in his shoulders releasing by incremental degrees as he exhaled slowly.

"This is either the smartest or the stupidest decision we've ever made," he muttered, holstering his sidearm with practiced efficiency. "And we've made some spectacularly questionable calls over the years."

Anna didn't respond immediately. Exhaustion had etched itself into the lines around her eyes, the shadows beneath them dark as bruises against her skin. Her shaved head felt cold in the dark.

"Let's get going," she said. "Tomorrow is a big day."

Epilogue:

They drove through the night and Anna leaned against Casper's shoulder, enjoying the warmth.

She knew what it was to be alone.

How often she'd endured it.

Now... strangely, it almost felt as if she were alone *with* someone, or rather, sharing the burden of loneliness with a similar soul.

Dawn broke over the Russian coastline, painting the slate-gray waters of the Baltic with molten gold. The SUV hugged the winding coastal road, its powerful engine humming a steady counterpoint to the rhythmic crash of waves against the rocky shore below. Anna watched the transformation of the world through half-lidded eyes, her head resting against Casper's solid shoulder.

The landscape unfurled before them like a dream rendered in watercolors—morning mist rising from dense pine forests that marched right to the cliff edges, occasional breaks revealing stretches of pristine beach where no human footprints marred the sand. Gulls wheeled overhead, their distant cries carried away by the salt-laden breeze that slipped through the vehicle's slightly opened windows.

Casper drove with the relaxed precision that characterized everything he did—hands positioned exactly at ten and two, eyes constantly scanning the road ahead while periodically checking the mirrors. The early light carved shadows beneath his cheekbones, emphasizing the weathered contours of a face that had witnessed too much, endured too much. Yet there was a peace to him now that had been absent during those tense moments in the forest clearing.

Anna's body swayed gently with the vehicle's movement, her muscles finally surrendering to the bone-deep exhaustion that followed extreme stress. The warmth of Casper's body beside her created a pocket of safety that allowed her vigilance to slip, just slightly, for the first time in days. Her tactical vest lay discarded in the footwell, the Albino's phone secured in her pocket, pressed against her thigh like a talisman.

They passed through a small fishing village, the inhabitants just beginning their day's work. Weathered boats painted in faded blues and reds bobbed in a natural harbor, nets spread across wooden racks to dry in the strengthening sunlight. An old woman looked up from sweeping her doorstep, her gaze following the unfamiliar vehicle with the mild curiosity of someone who had seen many strangers come and go across decades of quiet observation.

Neither spoke. Neither needed to. The silence between them was comfortable, built on years of shared experiences that transcended the necessity of words. Casper's breathing maintained its steady rhythm, a metronome that Anna found herself synchronizing with unconsciously. His shoulder rose and fell beneath her cheek, solid and dependable as the earth itself.

In the trunk, their dangerous passenger made no sound. The reinforced divider separated them from Kovac as effectively as if he were in another world entirely, though Anna remained acutely aware of his presence—a gravitational force that subtly altered the dynamics of their journey. Even silent, even contained, he exerted an influence that couldn't be ignored.

"The streak in your hair," Casper said suddenly, breaking the comfortable silence. His voice was low, almost gentle—a tone he reserved exclusively for their rare moments of safety. "I'm going to miss it."

"It'll grow back," she whispered.

"The new look suits you," he said after a moment, the ghost of a smile softening the hard lines of his face.

They fell back into silence as the road curved inland, the sea disappearing behind them as they entered denser forest. Pine shadows dappled the asphalt, creating a hypnotic pattern that seemed to pulse with the vehicle's movement. The SUV's navigation system indicated they were approaching their immediate destination—a safe house maintained by contacts Casper had cultivated during his years in private security.

"Anthony Starr," Casper said eventually, testing the name as if it were a foreign object he was examining for authenticity. "Four-star general. Presidential advisor. Architect of three major military campaigns. Supposedly died in a helicopter crash three years ago." His hands tightened imperceptibly on the steering wheel. "And now, apparently, trafficking children."

Anna straightened slightly, her moment of relaxation giving way to the sharp focus that the topic demanded. "The Albino's messages confirmed it. Starr is the buyer. Tomorrow's meeting was to finalize another transaction." She withdrew the phone from her pocket, its screen illuminating her face with cold electronic light. "Coordinates, security protocols, payment verification. All here."

Casper's expression hardened, the transition from companion to operator visible in the subtle realignment of his facial muscles. "You're sure it's him? Not someone using his identity as cover?"

"The Albino knew details," Anna replied, scrolling through messages on the phone. "Operational specifics that only someone with Starr's background would recognize. References to joint missions in theaters where Starr had commanded. It's him."

The implications hung between them, heavy as storm clouds. Anthony Starr had been a legend—a tactician whose strategies had reshaped modern warfare, a leader whose mere presence had supposedly changed the outcome of key conflicts. His private security firm, established after his retirement from active duty, had become the gold standard in the industry, securing contracts worth billions from governments and corporations worldwide.

And now he was purchasing children on the black market.

"If Starr is alive," Casper said, voice dropping to a dangerous rumble, "if he's involved in this... the implications go beyond human trafficking." He guided the SUV around a sharp curve, tires gripping the damp asphalt with reassuring tenacity. "A man with his connections, his knowledge of classified operations—"

"I don't care about the geopolitical implications," Anna cut him off, her voice acquiring the brittle edge that appeared whenever she discussed her missing family. "I care about finding Sarah and Tony."

Casper nodded once, accepting the rebuke without offense. "Of course." He reached over, patting her on the arm.

The two of them lapsed into silence then. The Albino was dead, one danger left lying in the cooling blood behind them—another now looming like the morning mist ahead of them, like the crooked road they now drove into the unknown.

What's Next for Anna?

Book 6 - Guardian's Vendetta

They took her family. Now she's bringing the war to their doorstep.

When ex–Navy SEAL and black ops legend Anna Gabriel gets word that her sister's children are being held on a remote U.S. military base in Turkey, she doesn't ask questions—she grabs her gear. The man behind the abduction? A ruthless American general who faked his own death and vanished into the shadows of a rogue operation.

Now he's back, running a covert facility off the grid, surrounded by soldiers loyal to his cause—and he's using Anna's family as leverage.

But he's about to learn what happens when you cross the wrong woman.

With her elite training, lethal instincts, and nothing left to lose, Anna launches a one-woman assault deep behind enemy lines. The mission: infiltrate the base, outwit an army, and extract the kids before they disappear forever.

This time, it's not about orders.It's not about justice.It's personal.

Also by Georgia Wagner

Once a rising star in the FBI, with the best case closure rate of any investigator, Ella Porter is now exiled to a small gold mining town bordering the wilderness of Alaska. The reason for her new assignment? She allowed a prolific serial killer to escape custody.

But what no one knows is that she did it on purpose.

The day she shows up in Nome, bags still unpacked, the wife of the richest gold miner in town goes missing. This is the second woman to vanish in as many days. And it's up to Ella to find out what happened.

Assigning Ella to Nome is no accident, either. Though she swore she'd never return, Ella grew up in the small, gold mining town, treated like royalty as a child due to her own family's wealth. But like all gold tycoons, the Porter family secrets are as dark as Ella's own.

Also by Georgia Wagner

The skeletons in her closet are twitching...

Genius chess master and FBI consultant Artemis Blythe swore she'd never return to the misty Cascade Mountains.

GUARDIAN'S MISSION

Her father—a notorious serial killer, responsible for the deaths of seven women—is now imprisoned, in no small part due to a clue she provided nearly fifteen years ago.

And now her father wants his vengeance.

A new serial killer is hunting the wealthy and the elite in the town of Pinelake. Artemis' father claims he knows the identity of the killer, but he'll only tell daughter dearest. Against her will, she finds herself forced back to her old stomping grounds.

Once known as a child chess prodigy, now the locals only think of her as 'The Ghostkiller's' daughter.

In the face of a shamed family name and a brother involved with the Seattle mob, Artemis endeavours to use her tactical genius to solve the baffling case.

Hunting a murderer who strikes without a trace, if she fails, the next skeleton in her closet will be her own.

Also by Georgia Wagner

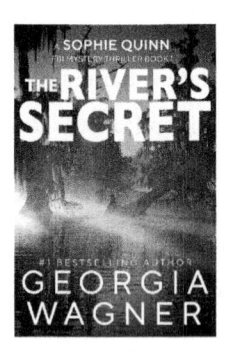

A cold knife, a brutal laugh.

Then the odds-defying escape.

Once a hypnotist with her own TV show, now, Sophie Quinn works as a full-time consultant for the FBI. Everything changed six years ago. She can still remember that horrible night. Slated to be the River Killer's tenth victim, she managed to slip her bindings and barely escape where so many others failed. Her sister wasn't so lucky.

And now the killer is back.

Two PHDs later, she's now a rising star at the FBI. Her photographic memory helps solve crimes, but also helps her to never forget. She saw the River Killer's tattoo. She knows what he sounds like. And now, ten years later, he's active again.

Sophie Quinn heads back home to the swamps of Louisiana, along the Mississippi River, intent on evening the score and finding the man who killed her sister. It's been six years since she's been home, though. Broken relationships and shattered dreams exist among the bayous, the rivers, the waterways and swamps of Louisiana; can Sophie find her way home again? Or will she be the River Killer's next victim to float downstream?

Want to know more?

Want to see what else the Greenfield authors have written? Go to the website.

https://greenfieldpress.co.uk/

Or sign up to our newsletter where you will get sneak peeks, exclusive giveaways, behind the scenes content, and more. Plus, you'll be notified of Fan Pricing events when they occur and get exclusive offers from other authors.

https://greenfieldpress.co.uk/newsletter/

Prefer social media? Join our thriving Facebook community.

Want to join the inner circle where you can keep up to date with everything? This is a free page on Facebook where you can hang out with likeminded individuals and enjoy discussing my books.

There is cake too (but only if you bring it).

https://www.facebook.com/GreenfieldPress

About the Author

Georgia Wagner worked as a ghost writer for many, many years before finally taking the plunge into self-publishing. Location and character are two big factors for Georgia, and getting those right allows the story to flow seamlessly onto the page. And flow it does, because Georgia is so prolific a new term is required to describe the rate at which nerve-tingling stories find their way into print.

When not found attached to a laptop, Georgia likes spending time in local arboretums, among the trees and ponds. An avid cultivator of orchids, begonias, and all things floral, Georgia also has a strong penchant for art, paintings, and sculptures.